A
SMALL CHILD'S
BOOK of VERSE

Compiled and Illustrated by
PELAGIE DOANE

New York
OXFORD UNIVERSITY PRESS
1948

To Warren

SEASONS
Holidays
ANiMALS
everyday experiences, moving

CONTENTS

Poetry

What is poetry? Who knows?
Not the rose, but the scent of the rose;
Not the sky, but the light of the sky;
Not the fly, but the gleam of the fly;
Not the sea, but the sound of the sea;
Not myself, but something that makes me
See, hear and feel something that prose
Cannot; what is it? Who knows?

ELEANOR FARJEON

JUST ABOUT ME

Song for a Little House

I'm glad our house is a little house,
    Not too tall nor too wide;
I'm glad the hovering butterflies
    Feel free to come inside.

Our little house is a friendly house,
    It is not shy or vain;
It gossips with the talking trees,
    And makes friends with the rain.

And quick leaves cast a shimmer of green
    Against our whited walls,
And in the phlox the courteous bees
    Are paying duty calls.

CHRISTOPHER MORLEY

Our House

I like our house because it is so big and old,
With lots of places where I can go and hide
When I want to . . .
And an attic I can shut myself inside.

My room has one high window where I watch
    the moon
Leaking through the maples, and making
The concrete walk look like a river
Right in our backyard—

A silver river with black fishes swimming
In the shadows—
Just alive with little black fishes shaking
In the silver water. . . .
It's funny that no one ever saw
That river before—
It drops out of sight at the basement door
I can hear it whispering under the floor,
It goes to China, I suppose,
But I'll never tell—and *nobody knows*
Only me.

I like our garden, too, it isn't set in rows,
But looks as if things happened just to grow
Right there that way. . . .
And if a hollyhock comes up by chance beside
    a rose,
Not close enough to choke,
My mother lets it stay.
Sometimes at night when it is white and still
The garden shivers till the poppies spill
Their petals on the grass,
And once I saw a shadow pass over it—
It wasn't a shadow exactly because it was light,
And it wasn't a wind because it was still—
It's funny that nobody saw it come over the hill
And stop in our garden—*nobody knows*
Only me and I'll never tell.

NELLIE BURGET MILLER

6

Fun in a Garret

We're having a lovely time to-day!
We're all of us up in the garret at play!
We have three houses under the eaves—
Not real, you know, but make-believes.
Two we live in, and one is a store,
Where a little old screen makes a truly door.

Warren keeps store, and Joe is his clerk.
And Betty and I stay home and work.
Joe comes around and knocks or rings,
And we order potatoes and steaks and things,
And sometimes we go to the store and buy,
Or send the children for ribbons or pie.

It's lots of fun—just try it some day
When it rains too hard to go out to play.

EMMA C. DOWD

The Cellar

I love my queer cellar with its dusty smell,
Its misty smell like smoke-fringes
From clouds blowing past;
With its shelves of jams and goodies,
With its boxes . . . barrels. . . .
Woodpiles here and there.
There is a passageway
To an unknown room
Where bins hold carrots and things.
There are glass doors that bang
And cobweb windows.
I love the quietness of my cellar
Thinking in the dark.
My cellar has apples in its breath,
Potatoes even,
That smell of earth.

HILDA CONKLING

7

The Cupboard

I know a little cupboard,
    With a teeny, tiny key,
And there's a jar of lollypops
    For me, me, me.

It has a little shelf, my dear,
    As dark as dark can be,
And there's a dish of Banbury Cakes,
    For me, me, me.

I have a small fat grandmamma,
    With a very slippery knee,
And she's the keeper of the Cupboard,
    With a key, key, key.

And when I'm very good, my dear,
    As good as good can be,
There's Banbury Cakes, and lollypops
    For me, me, me.

                    WALTER DE LA MARE

The Teapot Dragon

There's a dragon on our teapot,
    With a long and crinkly tail,
His claws are like a pincer-bug,
    His wings are like a sail;

His tongue is always sticking out,
    And so I used to think
He must be very hungry, or
    He wanted tea to drink.

But once when Mother wasn't round
    I dipped my fingers in,
And when I pulled them out I found
    I'd blistered all the skin.

Now when I see the dragon crawl
    Around our china pot,
I know he's burned his tongue because
    The water is so hot.

                    RUPERT SARGENT HOLLAND

A Coffeepot Face

I saw
my face
in the coffeepot.
Imagine,
a coffeepot face!

My cheeks
were big
and my nose was *not*,
And my mouth
was every place.

                    AILEEN FISHER

My Bed

I have a little bed
Just for me.
Brother's too big for it.
Mummy's too big for it.
Daddy's too big for it.
Do you see?

I have a little bed,
Do you see?
But—pussy's too small for it.
Puppy's too small for it.
Baby's too small for it.
It's just for me.

                    ELIZABETH MANSON SCOTT

8

A Song of Bread and Honey

Of all the meals you can buy for money,
Give me a meal of bread and honey!

A table of grass in the open air, ·
A green bank for an easy chair,

The table-cloth inwrought with flowers
And a grasshopper clock to tick the hours.

Between the courses the birds to sing
To many a hidden shining string.

And neither man nor maid be seen,
But a great company of green

Upon a hundred thousand stalks
Talk to us its great green talks.

And, when the merry meal is done,
To loiter westward with the sun,

Dipping fingers ere we go
In the stream that runs below.

Of all the meals you can buy for money
Give me a meal of bread and honey!

RICHARD LE GALLIENNE

Animal Crackers

Animal crackers, and cocoa to drink,
That is the finest of suppers, I think;
When I'm grown up and can have what I
    please
I think I shall always insist upon these.

What do you choose when you're offered a
    treat?
When Mother says, "What would you like best
    to eat?"
Is it waffles and syrup, or cinnamon toast?
It's cocoa and animals that *I* love the most!

The kitchen's the coziest place that I know:
The kettle is singing, the stove is aglow,
And there in the twilight, how jolly to see
The cocoa and animals waiting for me.

Daddy and Mother dine later in state,
With Mary to cook for them, Susan to wait;
But they don't have nearly as much fun as I
Who eat in the kitchen with Nurse standing
    by;
And Daddy once said, he would like to be me
Having cocoa and animals once more for tea!

CHRISTOPHER MORLEY

Shoes

My father has a pair of shoes
So beautiful to see!
I want to wear my father's shoes,
They are too big for me.

My baby brother has a pair,
As cunning as can be!
My feet won't go into that pair,
They are too small for me.

There's only one thing I can do
Till I get small or grown.
If I want to have a fitting shoe,
I'll have to wear my own.

TOM ROBINSON

New Shoes

When I am walking down the street
I do so like to watch my feet.
Perhaps you do not know the news,
Mother has bought me fine new shoes!
When the left one steps I do not speak,
I listen to its happy squeak.

MARJORIE SEYMOUR WATTS

New Shoes

I have new shoes in the Fall-time
And new ones in the Spring.
Whenever I wear my new shoes
I always have to sing!

ALICE WILKINS

Hair Ribbons

I'm three years old and like to wear,
A bow of ribbon on my hair.
Sometimes it's pink, sometimes it's blue;
I think it's pretty there, don't you?

UNKNOWN

My Zipper Suit

My zipper suit is bunny-brown—
The top zips up, the legs zip down.
I wear it every day.
My daddy brought it out from town.
Zip it up, and zip it down,
And hurry out to play!

MARIE LOUISE ALLEN

My paws are like a kitten's
When I wear my Sunday mittens
Which are lovely, fluffy white
Angora wool.

I can stretch them nice and wide,
So my thumb can come inside
To cuddle with my fingers,
When I pull.

A HOME-MADE JINGLE

William has some new pajamas,
Yellow cotton striped with brown,
And he says that when he wears them
He's a tiger lying down.

We are wakened in the morning
By a fearful, hungry roar
And the brown and yellow tiger
Plunges through our bedroom door.

He says he's going to eat us—
We are terrified! But then
The tiger peels his skin off—
He's our little boy again.

A HOME-MADE JINGLE

Smells (Junior)

My Daddy smells like tobacco and books,
　　Mother, like lavender and listerine;
Uncle John carries a whiff of cigars,
　　Nannie smells starchy and soapy and clean.

Shandy, my dog, has a smell of his own
　　(When he's been out in the rain he smells
　　　　most);
But Katie, the cook, is more splendid than all—
　　She smells exactly like hot buttered toast!

CHRISTOPHER MORLEY

Little

I am the sister of him
And he is my brother.
He is too little for us
To talk to each other.

So every morning I show him
My doll and my book;
But every morning he still is
Too little to look.

DOROTHY ALDIS

Little Brother's Secret

When my birthday was coming
Little Brother had a secret.
He kept it for days and days
And just hummed a little tune when I asked
　　him.
But one night it rained,
And I woke up and heard him crying;
Then he told me.
"I planted two lumps of sugar in your garden
Because you love it so frightfully.
I thought there would be a whole sugar tree for
　　your birthday.
And now it will be all melted."
Oh, the darling!

KATHERINE MANSFIELD

Experience

Deborah danced, when she was two,
As buttercups and daffodils do;

Spirited, frail, naïvely bold,
Her hair a ruffled crest of gold.
And whenever she spoke her voice went
　　singing
Like water up from a fountain springing.

But now her step is quiet and slow;
She walks the way the primroses go;
Her hair is yellow instead of gilt,
Her voice is losing its lovely lilt;
And in place of her wild delightful ways
A quaint precision rules her days.

For Deborah is now three, and, oh,
She knows so much that she did not know.

ALINE KILMER

Manners

I have an uncle I don't like,
　　An aunt I cannot bear:
She chucks me underneath the chin,
　　He ruffles up my hair.

Another uncle I adore,
　　Another aunty, too:
She shakes me kindly by the hand,
　　He says, "How do you do?"

MARIANA GRISWOLD VAN RENSSELAER

The Lost Doll

I once had a sweet little doll, dears,
  The prettiest doll in the world;
Her cheeks were so red and so white, dears,
  And her hair was so charmingly curled.
But I lost my poor little doll, dears,
  As I played on the heath one day;
And I cried for her more than a week, dears,
  But I never could find where she lay.

I found my poor little doll, dears,
  As I played on the heath one day;
Folks say she is terribly changed, dears,
  For her paint is all washed away,
And her arm trodden off by the cows, dears,
  And her hair not the least bit curled;
Yet for old time's sake, she is still, dears,
  The prettiest doll in the world.

CHARLES KINGSLEY

Doll Song

Matilda Jane, you never look
At any toy or picture-book:
I show you pretty things in vain—
You must be blind, Matilda Jane;

I ask you riddles, tell you tales,
But *all* our conversation fails:
You *never* answer me again—
I fear you're dumb, Matilda Jane;

Matilda, darling, when I call,
You never seem to hear at all:
I shout with all my might and main—
But you're *so* deaf, Matilda Jane!

Matilda Jane, you needn't mind:
For though you're deaf, and dumb, and blind,
There's *someone* loves you, it is plain—
And that is *me*, Matilda Jane!

LEWIS CARROLL

The Invisible Playmate

When the other children go,
    Though there's no one seems to see
And there's no one seems to know,
    Fanny comes and plays with me.

She has yellow curly hair
    And her dress is always blue.
And she always plays quite fair
    Everything I tell her to.

People say she isn't there—
    They step over her at play
And they sit down in her chair
    In the very rudest way.

It is queer they cannot know
    When she's there for me to see!
When the other children go
    Fanny comes and plays with me.

MARGARET WIDDEMER

Playgrounds

In summer I am very glad
    We children are so small,
For we can see a thousand things
    That men can't see at all.

They don't know much about the moss
    And all the stones they pass;
They never lie and play among
    The forests in the grass.

They walk about a great way off;
    And, when we're at the sea,
Let father stoop as best he can,
    He can't find things like me.

But when the snow is on the ground
    And all the puddles freeze,
I wish that I were very tall,
    High up above the trees.

LAWRENCE ALMA-TADEMA

Camp Chums

Good-by, schoolhouse! Good-by, books!
My pocket's full of fishing hooks;
I've found my old last year's straw hat,
My swimming suit and baseball bat.
I'm going to Grandma's house next week
And swim all summer in Sugar Creek.
And whether it shines or whether it pours
Grandpa and I are going to live outdoors.
We'll cook by the campfire, and talk about
When I'm old enough to be a scout,
And we don't want to be in a house at all
Till the school bell rings again next fall.

ROSE WALDO

13

Skating

When I try to skate,
My feet are so wary
They grit and they grate:
And then I watch Mary
Easily gliding,
Like an ice-fairy;
Skimming and curving,
Out and in,
With a turn of her head,
And a lift of her chin,
And a gleam of her eye,
And a twirl and a spin;
Sailing under
The breathless hush
Of the willows, and back
To the frozen rush;
Out to the island
And round the edge,
Skirting the rim
Of the crackling sedge,
Swerving close
To the poplar root,
And round the lake
On a single foot,

With a three, and an eight,
And a loop and a ring;
Where Mary glides,
The lake will sing!
Out in the mist
I hear her now
Under the frost
Of the willow-bough
Easily sailing,
Light and fleet,
With the song of the lake
Beneath her feet.

HERBERT ASQUITH

Icy

I slip and I slide
On the slippery ice;
I skid and I glide,—
Oh, isn't it nice
To lie on your tummy
And slither and skim
On the slick crust of snow
Where you skid as you swim?

RHODA W. BACMEISTER

14

Swing Song

Swing, swing,
Sing, sing
Here's my throne, and I am a King!
Swing, sing,
Swing, sing,
Farewell earth, for I'm on the wing!

Low, high,
Here I fly,
Like a bird through sunny sky;
Free, free
Over the lea,
Over the mountain, over the sea!

Up, down,
Up and down,
Which is the way to London Town?
Where, where?
Up in the air,
Close your eyes, and now you are there!

Soon, soon,
Afternoon,
Over the sunset, over the moon;
Far, far
Over all bar,
Sweeping on from star to star!

No, no,
Low, low,
Sweeping daisies with my toe.
Slow, slow,
To and fro,
Slow——
    slow——
        slow——
            slow.

WILLIAM ALLINGHAM

Extremes

A little boy once played so loud
That the Thunder, up in a thunder-cloud,
Said, "Since I can't be heard, why, then,
I'll never, never thunder again!"

And a little girl once kept so still
That she heard a fly on the window-sill
Whisper and say to a lady-bird,
"She's the stilliest child I ever heard!"

JAMES WHITCOMB RILEY

Gentle Name

Mary is a gentle name
Like the sound of silver bells,
Like a blue and quiet flame,
Like country brooks and ferny smells;
A friendly, wistful name and airy—
Mary

SELMA ROBINSON

An Indignant Male

The way they scrub
Me in the tub,
I think there's
    Hardly
    Any
    Doubt
Sometime they'll rub
And rub and rub
Until they simply
    Rub
    Me
    Out.

A. B. ROSS

15

Mud Cakes

(A GOOD RECIPE)

Some water—about a half a cup—
And two full cups of earth,
Mix well and beat and beat and beat
For all that you are worth:
Roll out and cut a half inch thick—
A dozen or so 'twill make,
Then arrange them on a board
And set in sun to bake!

FROSTING

A cup of sand, the white is best,
Add water drop by drop
Until enough to mix and spread
All over each cake top!
In center stick a big, fat plum
Or a berry or a cherry meat
And then you'll have some little cakes
That *look* good enough to eat!

MILDRED D. SHACKLETT

Swimming

When all the days are hot and long
And robin bird has ceased his song,
I go swimming every day
And have the finest kind of play.

I've learned to dive and I can float
As easily as does a boat;
I splash and plunge and laugh and shout
Till Daddy tells me to come out.

It's much too soon—I'd like to cry—
For I can see the ducks go by,
And Daddy Duck—how I love him—
He lets his children swim and swim!

I feel that I would be in luck
If I could only be a duck!

CLINTON SCOLLARD

Mud

Mud is very nice to feel
   All squishy-squash between the toes!
I'd rather wade in wiggly mud
   Than smell a yellow rose.

Nobody else but the rosebush knows
How nice mud feels
   Between the toes.

POLLY CHASE BOYDEN

Mumps

I had a feeling in my neck,
    And on the sides were two big bumps;
I couldn't swallow anything
    At all because I had the mumps.

And Mother tied it with a piece.
    And then she tied up Will and John,
And no one else but Dick was left
    That didn't have a mump rag on.

He teased at us and laughed at us,
    And said, whenever he went by,
"It's vinegar and lemon drops
    And pickles!" just to make us cry.

But Tuesday Dick was very sad
    And cried because his neck was sore,
And not a one said sour things
    To anybody any more.

ELIZABETH MADOX ROBERTS

Whistle

I want to learn to whistle,
I've always wanted to;
I fix my mouth to do it, but
The whistle won't come through.

I think perhaps it's stuck, and so
I try it once again;
Can people swallow whistles?
Where is my whistle then?

DOROTHY ALDIS

Sprinkling

Sometimes in the summer
When the day is hot
Daddy takes the garden hose
And finds a shady spot;
Then he calls me over
Looks at my bare toes
And says, "Why, you need sprinkling,
You thirsty little rose!"

DOROTHY MASON PIERCE

Sneezing

Air comes in tickly
Through my nose,
Then very quickly—
Out it goes:
Ahhh — CHOO!

With every sneeze
I have to do,
I make a breeze—
Ahh — CHOO! — Ahh — CHOO!

MARY LOUISE ALLEN

17

The First Tooth

There once was a wood, and a very thick wood,
So thick that to walk was as much as you could;
But a sunbeam got in, and the trees understood.

I went to this wood, at the end of the snows,
And as I was walking I saw a primrose;
Only one! Shall I show you the place where it
    grows?

There once was a house, and a very dark house,
As dark, I believe, as the hole of a mouse,
Or a tree in my wood, at the thick of the
    boughs.

I went to this house, and I searched it aright,
I opened the chambers, and I found a light;
Only one! Shall I show you this little lamp
    bright?

There once was a cove, and this very dark cave
One day took a gift from an incoming wave;
And I made up my mind to know what the sea
    gave.

I took a lit torch, I walked round the ness
When the water was lowest; and in a recess
In my cave was a jewel. Will nobody guess?

O there was a baby, he sat on my knee,
With a pearl in his mouth that was precious to
    me,
His little dark mouth like my cave of the sea!

I said to my heart, "And my jewel is bright!
He blooms like a primrose! He shines like a
    light!"
Put your hand in his mouth! Do you feel? He
    can bite!

WILLIAM BRIGHTY RANDS

Walking

When Daddy
Walks
With Jean and me,
We have a
Lot of fun
'Cause we can't
Walk as fast
As he,
Unless we
Skip and
Run!
I stretch,
And stretch
My legs so far,
I nearly slip
And fall—
But how
Does Daddy
Take such steps?
He doesn't stretch
At all!

GRACE GLAUBITZ

Funny

When you stop to think of it, isn't it funny
The wiggle-y nose that there is on a bunny,
The smartness of bees to know all about honey,
The difference in days that are rainy or sunny,
The way that our legs can be walky or runny—
When you stop to think of it, isn't it funny?

AILEEN FISHER

18

ALL THROUGH THE YEAR

The Garden Year

January brings the snow,
Makes our feet and fingers glow.

February brings the rain,
Thaws the frozen lake again.

March brings breezes, loud and shrill,
To stir the dancing daffodil.

April brings the primrose sweet,
Scatters daisies at our feet.

May brings flocks of pretty lambs
Skipping by their fleecy dams.

June brings tulips, lilies, roses,
Fills the children's hands with posies.

Hot July brings cooling showers,
Apricots, and gillyflowers.

August brings the sheaves of corn,
Then the harvest home is borne.

Warm September brings the fruit;
Sportsmen then begin to shoot.

Fresh October brings the pheasant;
Then to gather nuts is pleasant.

Dull November brings the blast;
Then the leaves are whirling fast.

Chill December brings the sleet,
Blazing fire, and Christmas treat.

SARA COLERIDGE

Winter

Bread and milk for breakfast,
    And woolen frocks to wear,
And a crumb for robin redbreast
    On the cold days of the year.

CHRISTINA ROSSETTI

The New Year

Who comes dancing over the snow,
    His soft little feet all bare and rosy?
Open the door, though the wild winds blow,
    Take the child in and make him cozy.
Take him in and hold him dear
He is the wonderful glad New Year.

DINAH MARIA MULOCK CRAIK

20

Song

Tomorrow is Saint Valentine's day,
    All in the morning betime,
And I a maid at your window
    To be your Valentine.

WILLIAM SHAKESPEARE

A Valentine

Frost flowers on the window glass,
Hopping chickadees that pass,
Bare old elms that bend and sway,
Pussywillows soft and gray,

Silver clouds across the sky,
Lacy snowflakes flitting by,
Icicles like fringe in line—
That is Outdoor's valentine!

ELEANOR HAMMOND

The Address

I wonder if the name is right—
    I guess 'twill have to do,
I didn't know exactly how
    So I spelled it Y-O-U.

OLD VALENTINE

Hearts and Lace Paper

Lilies are white, rosemary's green;
When you are king, I will be queen.

Roses are red, violets blue,
If you will have me, I will have you.

To My Valentine

If apples were pears,
And peaches were plums,
And the rose had a different name,—
If tigers were bears,
And fingers were thumbs,
I'd love you just the same!

AUTHOR UNKNOWN

A Sure Sign

Here's the mail, sort it quick—
Papers, letters, notes,
Postcard scenes,
Magazines;
Our hearts are in our throats.
Something there,
White and square,
Sealed with wax, and bumpy—
At the edges flat and thin,
In the middle lumpy?
When you feel the envelope,
Do your fingers trace
Something narrow,
Like an arrow?
Or a part
Of a heart?
Or a Cupid's face?
Is your name across the back
In a crooked line?
Hurry, then; that's a sign
Someone's sent a valentine!

NANCY BYRD TURNER

21

The March Wind ✔

I come to work as well as play;
  I'll tell you what I do;
I whistle all the live-long day,
  "Woo-oo-oo-oo! Woo-oo!"

I toss the branches up and down
  And shake them to and fro,
I whirl the leaves in flocks of brown,
  And send them high and low.

I strew the twigs upon the ground,
  The frozen earth I sweep;
I blow the children round and round
  And wake the flowers from sleep.

UNKNOWN

Wind Is a Cat

Wind is a cat
  That prowls at night,
Now in a valley,
  Now on a height,

Pouncing on houses
  Till folks in their beds
Draw all the covers
  Over their heads.

It sings to the moon,
  It scratches at doors;
It lashes its tail
  Around chimneys and roars.

It claws at the clouds
  Till it fringes their silk,
It laps up the dawn
  Like a saucer of milk;

Then, chasing the stars
  To the tops of the firs,
Curls down for a nap
  And purrs and purrs.

ETHEL ROMIG FULLER

I saw the wind to-day:
I saw it in the pane
Of glass upon the wall:
A moving thing,—'twas like
No bird with widening wing,
No mouse that runs along
The meal bag under the beam.

I think it like a horse,
All black, with frightening mane,
That springs out of the earth,
And tramples on his way.
I saw it in the glass,
The shaking of a mane:
A horse that no one rides!

PADRAIC COLUM

The Wind

Why does the wind so want to be
Here in my little room with me?
He's all the world to blow about,
But just because I keep him out
He cannot be a moment still,
But frets upon my window sill,
And sometimes brings a noisy rain
To help him batter at the pane.

Upon my door he comes to knock.
He rattles, rattles at the lock
And lifts the latch and stirs the key—
Then waits a moment breathlessly,
And soon, more fiercely than before,
He shakes my little trembling door,
And though "Come in, come in!" I say,
He neither comes nor goes away.

Barefoot across the chilly floor
I run and open wide the door;
He rushes in and back again
He goes to batter door and pane,
Pleased to have blown my candle out.
He's all the world to blow about,
Why does he want so much to be
Here in my little room with me?

ELIZABETH RENDALL

I Heard It in the Valley

I heard it in the valley,
I heard it in the glen;
Listen, children, surely, surely
Spring is coming back again!

I heard it in the valley,
I heard it on the hill,
I heard it where the bare trees stand,
Very brave and still.

I heard it in the valley—
I heard the waters start,
I heard it surely, surely,
I heard it in my heart!

ANNETTE WYNNE

Wise Johnny

Little Johnny-jump-up said,
"It must be spring,
I just saw a lady-bug
And heard a robin sing."

EDWINA FALLIS

Song ✓

The year's at the spring,
And day's at the morn;
Morning's at seven;
The hill-side's dew-pearled;
The lark's on the wing;
The snail's on the thorn;
God's in His Heaven—
All's right with the world!

ROBERT BROWNING

A Spring Message

I heard the rain fall in the night;
Softly it fell,
Slowly, carelessly,
And I knew
That everywhere little brown doors were
    opening,
That everywhere little green things were
    stepping
Shyly, daintily,
Over the threshold of Spring.

JOAN ALPERMANN

23

Spring

In the Spring,
Ting-a-ling,
In the Spring,
Ting-a-ling,
The merry little,
Merry little
Birdies sing;
With a "Chink, chink, chink!"
And a "Chirra-wira-wink!"
Till the wild green woods
With their music ring.

In the Spring,
Ting-a-ling,
In the Spring,
Ting-a-ling,
The merry little,
Merry little
Wild flowers spring.
'Tis a violet here,
And a mayflower there,
Till the wild green woods
Are a-bloom so fair.

In the Spring,
Ting-a-ling,
In the Spring,
Ting-a-ling,
The merry little children
Come and dance in a ring.
And the bluebells chime
To their dancing time,
And the birds join the words
With their sing song sing.

LAURA E. RICHARDS

Mirrors

Puddles in the street
Are mirrors at my feet
Shiny mirrors
Showing
Sky
And clouds
And trees
Still mirrors
Showing
Shimmering
Leaves.
Puddles in the street
Are mirrors at my feet
If I step
Carefully
I shall be
Very high
In the sky
With clouds
And trees
And shimmering
Leaves.
This mirror will not crack
If I step
Carefully
I only
Leave there
A ruffled track
Very high
In the sky
With clouds
And trees
And shimmering
Leaves.

Very Lovely

Wouldn't it be lovely if the rain came down
Till the water was quite high over all the town?
If the cabs and busses all were set afloat.
And we had to go to school in a little boat?

Wouldn't it be lovely if it still should pour
And we all went up to live on the second floor?
If we saw the butcher sailing up the hill,
And we took the letters in at the window sill?

It's been raining, raining, all the afternoon;
All these things might happen really very soon.
If we woke to-morrow and found they had
      begun,
Wouldn't it be glorious? *Wouldn't* it be fun?

ROSE FYLEMAN

The Rains of Spring

The rains of spring
Which hang to the branches
   Of the green willow,
Look like pearls upon a string.

LADY ISE ABOUT 1000 A.D.

A Shower

Shower came;
In I came;
Blue sky came!

IZEMBO. D. 1710

A Memory

Four ducks on a pond,
A grass-bank beyond,
A blue sky of spring,
White clouds on the wing;
What a little thing
To remember for years—
To remember with tears!

WILLIAM ALLINGHAM

Rain-Talk

Rain, Rain,
Are you there yet?

      Again, my pet.

Rain, Rain,
Why do you tap the pane?

      Let me come in.
      My feet are wet,
      I'm cold and thin,
      Let me come in!

I cannot let you in, I fear,
For mother has just barred the door,
And shut the windows. She does not hear.
Neither did I, perhaps, before.

      Then I'll stay out
      And rain all night.
      What are folks about?
      My coat's a sight!

RAELENE NEWELL WHITE

If Easter Eggs Would Hatch ✓

I wish that Easter eggs would do
   Like eggs of other seasons:
I wish that they hatched something, too,
   For—well, for lots of reasons.
The eggs you get the usual way
   Are always brown and white ones,
The eggs you find on Easter Day
   Are always gay and bright ones.

I'd love to see a purple hen,
   A rooster like a bluebird,
For that would make an old bird then
   Look really like a new bird.
If Easter eggs hatched like the rest,
   The robin and the swallow
Would peek inside a chicken's nest
   To see what styles to follow.

The rooster now is pretty proud,
   But wouldn't he be merry
If roosters only were allowed
   To dress like some canary!
And wouldn't it be fun to catch
   A little silver bunny!
If Easter eggs would only hatch,
   My, wouldn't that be funny!

DOUGLAS MALLOCH

Some Things That Easter Brings ✓

Easter duck and Easter chick,
Easter eggs with chocolate thick.

Easter hats for one and all,
Easter Bunny makes a call!

Happy Easter always brings
Such a lot of pleasant things.

ELSIE PARRISH

Easter

The air is like a butterfly
   With frail blue wings,
The happy earth looks at the sky
   And sings.

JOYCE KILMER

The Donkey

When fishes flew and forests walked
   And figs grew upon thorn,
Some moment when the moon was blood
   Then surely I was born;

With monstrous head and sickening cry
   And ears like errant wings,
The devil's walking parody
   On all four-footed things.

The tattered outlaw of the earth,
   Of ancient crooked will;
Starve, scourge, deride me: I am dumb,
   I keep my secret still.

Fools! For I also had my hour;
   One far fierce hour and sweet:
There was a shout about my ears,
   And palms before my feet.

GILBERT KEITH CHESTERTON

27

April

Something tapped at my windowpane,
   Someone called me without my door,
Someone laughed like the tinkle o'rain,
   The robin echoed it o'er and o'er.

I threw the door and the window wide;
   She, and the touch of the breeze, and then—
"Ah, were you expecting me, dear?" she cried,
   And here was April come back again.

THEODOSIA PICKERING GARRISON

Two little clouds one April day
   Went sailing across the sky.
They went so fast that they bumped their
     heads,
   And both began to cry.

The big round sun came out and said,
   "Oh, never mind, my dears,
I'll send all my sunbeams down
   To dry your fallen tears."

UNKNOWN

April Fool

Small April sobbed,
   "I'm going to cry!
Please give me a cloud
   To wipe my eye!"

Then, "April fool!"
   She laughed instead
And smiled a rainbow
   Overhead!

ELEANOR HAMMOND

The Day Before April

The day before April
   Alone, alone,
I walked in the woods
   And sat on a stone.

I sat on a broad stone
   And sang to the birds.
The tune was God's making
   But I made the words.

MARY CAROLYN DAVIES

April

April is a little girl
In a green poke bonnet
With a pompom daffodil
Nodding gaily on it.

April is a little girl
Shy as any starling—
Why the tears between the smiles?
Where's your hanky, darling?

EVELYN STOCKMAN

Sing-Time

Robin, sing to the rainbow!
Song-thrush, sing to the blue!
Springtime is on the hilltops
And all the world is new!

Winter slipped out through the valley
Where the pink and purple haze is;
And here is April with her arms
A-brimming full of daisies!

ROSE WALDO

April and May

April is a laundress
Mixing silver suds
To rinse the lacy dance frocks
Of apple-blossom buds.

May Day is the nursemaid
Who looks the flowers over
And ties their little bonnets
On the buttercup and clover.

ANNE ROBINSON

May

Merry, rollicking, frolicking May
Into the woods came skipping one day;
She teased the brook till he laughed outright,
And gurgled and scolded with all his might;
She chirped to the birds and bade them sing
A chorus of welcome to Lady Spring;
And the bees and the butterflies she set
To waking the flowers that were sleeping yet.
She shook the trees till the buds looked out
To see what the trouble was all about,
And nothing in Nature escaped that day
The touch of the life-giving bright young May.

GEORGE MACDONALD

Summer is coming! Summer is coming!
    How do you think I know?
I found some pussy willows
    So I know it must be so.

UNKNOWN

The Throstle

"Summer is coming, summer is coming,
    I know it, I know it, I know it.
Light again, leaf again, life again, love again,"
    Yes, my wild little Poet.

Sing the new year in under the blue.
    Last year you sang it as gladly.
"New, new, new, new!" Is it then *so* new
    That you should carol so madly?

"Love again, song again, nest again, young
    again,"
    Never a prophet so crazy!
And hardly a daisy as yet, little friend,
    See, there is hardly a daisy.

"Here again, here, here, here, happy year!"
    O warble unchidden, unbidden!
Summer is coming, is coming, my dear,
    And all the winters are hidden.

ALFRED TENNYSON

Laughing Song ‿

When the green woods laugh with the voice of
    joy,
And the dimpling stream runs laughing by;
When the air does laugh with our merry wit,
And the green hill laughs with the noise of it;

When the meadows laugh with lively green,
And the grasshopper laughs in the merry scene,
When Mary and Susan and Emily
With their sweet round mouth sang "Ha, Ha,
    He!"

When the painted birds laugh in the shade,
Where our table with cherries and nuts is
    spread,
Come live and be merry, and join with me,
To sing the sweet chorus of "Ha, Ha, He!"

WILLIAM BLAKE

September

A road like brown ribbon,
A sky that is blue,
A forest of green
With that sky peeping through.

Asters, deep purple,
A grasshopper's call,
Today it is summer,
Tomorrow is fall.

EDWINA FALLIS

September

Crickets are making
  The merriest din,
All the fields waking
  With shrill violin.

Now all the swallows
  Debate when to go;
In the valleys and hollows
  The mists are like snow.

Dahlias are glowing
  In purple and red
Where once were growing
  Pale roses instead.

Piled up leaves smoulder,
  All hazy the noon,
Nights have grown colder,
  The frost will come soon.

Early lamps burning,
  So soon the night falls,
Leaves, crimson turning,
  Make bright the stone walls.

Summer recalling
  At turn of the year,
Fruit will be falling,
  September is here.

EDWARD BLISS REED

September

The goldenrod is yellow,
  The corn is turning brown,
The trees in apple orchards
  With fruit are bending down.
The gentian's bluest fringes
  Are curling in the sun,
In dusty pods the milkweed
  Its hidden silk has spun.
The sedges flaunt their harvest
  In every meadow nook,
And asters by the brookside
  Make asters in the brook.
By all these lovely tokens
  September days are here,
With summer's best of weather
  And autumn's best of cheer.

HELEN HUNT JACKSON

In September

I walked down the lane
  Past the maple tree,
And Post Man wind
  Brought a note to me—
A small yellow note
  From my friend the tree!

You call it a "leaf"
  Just drifting down?
Why, it says, "Old Winter
  Will soon be in town!"
So it's really a letter
  The tree sent down!

ELEANOR HAMMOND

A Vagabond Song

There is something in the autumn that is native
    to my blood—
Touch of manner, hint of mood;
And my heart is like a rhyme,
With the yellow and the purple and the
    crimson keeping time.

The scarlet of the maples can shake me like
    a cry
Of bugles going by.
And my lonely spirit thrills
To see the frosty asters like a smoke upon
    the hills.

There is something in October sets the gypsy
    blood astir;
We must rise and follow her,
When from every hill of flame
She calls and calls each vagabond by name.

BLISS CARMAN

Theme in Yellow

I spot the hills
With yellow balls in autumn.
I light the prairie cornfields
Orange and tawny gold clusters
And I am called pumpkins.
On the last of October
When dusk is fallen
Children join hands
And circle round me
Singing ghost songs
And love to the harvest moon;
I am a jack-o'-lantern
With terrible teeth
And the children know
I am fooling.

CARL SANDBURG

32

Hallowe'en

Hallowe'en's the time for nuts
   And for apples, too,
And for funny faces that
   Stare and glare at you.
Right behind them is a friend,
   Jack or Bob or Bess
Isn't it the greatest fun
   When you try to guess?

               ANNA MEDARY

Black and Gold

Everything is black and gold,
   Black and gold, tonight:
Yellow pumpkins, yellow moon,
   Yellow candlelight;

Jet-black cat with golden eyes,
   Shadows black as ink,
Firelight blinking in the dark
   With a yellow blink.

Black and gold, black and gold,
   Nothing in between—
When the world turns black and gold,
   Then it's Hallowe'en!

            NANCY BYRD TURNER

Smiling

I met a Jack-o'-Lantern, Hallowe'en,
With the saddest face that I have ever seen!
For his mouth was turning down,
Both his eyes were made to frown,
And his forehead wrinkled crossly in between.

I thought it such a pity that his style
Had to keep him so unhappy all the while,
For, as everybody knows,
Just the nicest thing that grows
Anywhere, on anybody, is a smile.

               DIXIE WILLSON

If You've Never

If you've never seen an old witch
Riding through the sky—
Or never felt big bat's wings
Flopping, as they fly—
If you've never touched a white thing
Gliding through the air,
And knew it was a ghost because
You got a dreadful scare—
If you've never heard the night owls,
Crying, "Whoo-whoo-whoo?"
And never jumped at pumpkin eyes
Gleaming out at you—
If all of these exciting things
You've never heard nor seen,
Why then—you've missed a lot of fun,
Because—that's *Hallowe'en!*

               ELSIE M. FOWLER

33

November Night

Listen . . .
With faint dry sound,
Like steps of passing ghosts,
The leaves, frost-crisp'd, break from the trees
And fall.

ADELAIDE CRAPSEY

Autumn Leaves

The leaves are dropping from the trees,
    Yellow, brown and red.
They patter softly like the rain—
    One landed on my head!

But when the sleep of winter comes
    They cuddle down to rest;
Then Mother Nature tucks them in
    With snow as she thinks best.

MARGARET P. SUTPHEN (age 7)

Thanksgiving

The turkey is my favorite bird,
And mince my favorite pie,
And cranberry my favorite sauce—
    I wonder why?
I'm thankful for them all—aren't you?
And for the stuffing too!

MARGARET MUNSTERBERG

Autumn Woods

I like the woods
    In autumn
When dry leaves hide the ground,
When the trees are bare
And the wind sweeps by
With a lonesome rushing sound.

I can rustle the leaves
    In autumn
And I can make a bed
In the thick dry leaves
That have fallen
From the bare trees
Overhead.

JAMES S. TIPPETT

Cover

Red leaves flutter,
Yellow leaves fall,
Brown leaves gather
Along a wall.

Brown leaves huddle
Against the grey
Stones some farmer
Set one way

Between two pastures.
Curled leaves keep
Any wall warm
When winter's deep.

FRANCES M. FROST

34

The Best Time of All

Green for April, pink for June
    Red and gold for Fall,
But sparkly white for Wintertime,
    The best time of all.

Sing a song of Wintertime—
    Another freezing night,
And all the ruffly, ripply pond
    Is hard and crystal bright.

Then—one to stand and two to start,
    And three—away, away,
With zing! and zoon! Oh, what a tune
    The old pond sings today!

Sing a song of Wintertime,
    Of very trustful birds
Dropping in to call at noon,
    Full of friendly words.

Sing a song of Wintertime,
    A schoolyard full of snow,
Four-and-twenty fleecy tons
    Sifted high and sifted low.

We made a stoutish gentleman
    Before the morning session,
With buttons down his handsome front
    And such a pleased expression.

He slumped a little when it thawed
    And slimmer seemed to grow;
We liked him—and his pleasant grin
    Was last of all to go.

Snowballs rolling on and on,
    Swelling as they go;
Just how big a ball can get
    Only giants know.

Sing a song of snow and ice;
    Rime a dozen rimes;
Nippy, skippy Wintertime
    Is Best of all the times!

NANCY BYRD TURNER

Snow on the Roof

When we came to school today,
There was snow on the roof,
Snow on the boxes,
Snow on the blocks,
Snow on the boards,
Snow on the stairs.
There was snow all around us,
But nobody cared.

We took the brooms and shovels,
We cleaned off the roof.
We shoveled off the boxes,
We swept off the blocks,
We shoveled off the boards,
We swept off the stairs.
Now we have snow all over us,
But nobody cares!

ELIZABETH MANSON SCOTT

Jack Frost

Someone painted pictures on my
 Windowpane last night—
Willow trees with trailing boughs
 And flowers, frosty white,

And lovely crystal butterflies;
 But when the morning sun
Touched them with its golden beams,
 They vanished one by one!

HELEN BAYLEY DAVIS

A Story in the Snow

This morning, as I walked to school
 Across the fluffy snow,
I came upon a bunny's tracks—
 A jumping, zigzag row.

He must have hurried very fast,
 For here and there I saw
Along his jerky, winding trail
 The print of Rover's paw!

I set my lunch pail on the snow
 And stood there very still,
For only Rover's clumsy tracks
 Led down the little hill.

Then suddenly I thought I heard
 A rustling sound close by;
And there within a grassy clump
 Shone Bunny's twinkling eye!

PEARL RIGGS CROUCH

The Snowman's Resolution

The snowman's hat was crooked
 And his nose was out of place
And several of his whiskers
 Had fallen from his face.

But the snowman didn't notice
 For he was trying to think
Of a New Year's resolution
 That wouldn't melt or shrink.

He thought and planned and pondered
 With his little snow-ball head
Till his eyes began to glisten
 And his toes began to spread;

And at last he said, "I've got it—
 I'll make a firm resolve
That no matter what the weather
 My smile will not dissolve."

But the snowman acted wisely
 And his resolution won
For his splinter smile was wooden
 And it didn't mind the sun!

AILEEN FISHER

36

Galoshes

Susie's galoshes
Make splishes and sploshes
And slooshes and sloshes,
As Susie steps slowly
Along in the slush.

They stamp and they tramp
On the ice and concrete,
They get stuck in the muck and the mud;
But Susie likes much best to hear

The slippery slush
As it slooshes and sloshes,
And splishes and sploshes,
All round her galoshes!

RHODA W. BACMEISTER

Snowstorm

Oh, did you see the snow come?
  So softly floating down,—
White in the air, white on the trees,
  And white all over the ground!

It rattled gently on dry leaves;
  It tickled on my face;
And spread its thick, soft cover
  On every kind of place.

The autos standing in the street
  Had snowy tops and lights,
And even on my mummy's hat
  Was a big thick pile of white!

RHODA W. BACMEISTER

Snow-Flakes

Whenever a snow-flake leaves the sky,
It turns and turns to say "Good-bye!
Good-bye, dear cloud, so cool and gray!"
Then lightly travels on its way.

And when a snow-flake finds a tree,
"Good-day!" it says—"Good-day to thee!
Thou art so bare and lonely, dear,
I'll rest and call my comrades here."

But when a snow-flake, brave and meek,
Lights on a rosy maiden's cheek,
It starts—"How warm and soft the day!
'Tis summer!"—and it melts away.

MARY MAPES DODGE

The Little Red Sled

"Come out with me!" cried the little red sled.
"I'll give you the wings of a bird," it said.
"The ground is all snowy;
The wind is all blowy!
We'll go like a fairy,
So light and so airy!"

JOCELYN BUSH

Willows in the Snow

The willows hanging low,
Shake from their long and trailing skirts
  The freshly fallen snow.

TSURU

The Sleepy Maple Trees

I think they must be sorry—
  The little maple trees—
That they go to bed too early to
  See holidays like these!

They never see Thanksgiving
  Nor Hallowe'en at all,
Because they all go fast asleep
  So early in the fall.

Poor little tired maples,
  Sleeping in the breeze,
They miss the greatest fun of all—
  They can't be Christmas trees!

ELEANOR HAMMOND

Ambition ✓

Don't you think the trees remember
What day happens in December:
Hardly rustling, lest they should
Fail at being green and good;
Asking other shrubs that wait,
"Tell me, are my needles straight?"
Each one hoping, Oh, to be
Chosen for a Christmas Tree.

ANNE BLACKWELL PAYNE

I Heard a Bird Sing

I heard a bird sing
  In the dark of December
A magical thing
  And sweet to remember.

"We are nearer to Spring
  Than we were in September,"
I heard a bird sing
  In the dark of December.

OLIVER HERFORD

Bundles ✓

A bundle is a funny thing,
It always sets me wondering:
For whether it is thin or wide
You never know just what's inside.

Especially in Christmas week
Temptation is so great to peek!
Now wouldn't it be much more fun
If shoppers carried things undone?

JOHN FARRAR

The Twenty-fourth of December

The clock ticks slowly, slowly in the hall,
And slower and more slow the long hours
    crawl;
It seems as though to-day
Would never pass away;
The clock ticks slowly, s-l-o-w-l-y in the hall.

AUTHOR UNKNOWN

The Christmas Tree in the Nursery

With wild surprise
Four great eyes
In two small heads
From neighboring beds
Looked out—and winked—
And glittered and blinked
At a very queer sight
In the dim dawn-light.
As plain as can be
A fairy tree
Flashes and glimmers
And shakes and shimmers.
Red, green, and blue
Meet their view;
Silver and gold
Sharp eyes behold;
Small moons, big stars;
And jams in jars,
And cakes, and honey,
And thimbles, and money,
Pink dogs, blue cats,
Little squeaking rats,
And candles, and dolls,

And crackers, and polls,
A real bird that sings,
And tokens and favors,
And all sorts of things
For the little shavers.

Four black eyes
Grow big with surprise;
And then grow bigger
When a tiny figure,
Jaunty and airy,
A fairy! a fairy!
From the tree-top cries,
"Open wide! Black Eyes!
Come, children, wake now!
Your joys you may take now!"

Quick as you can think
  Twenty small toes
  In four pretty rows,
Like little piggies pink,
  All kick in the air—
And before you can wink
  The tree stands bare!

RICHARD WATSON GILDER

39

Juniper

Who does not love the juniper tree?
The scent of its branches comes back to me,
And ever I think of the Holy Tree
Who came to rest by the juniper tree.
Joseph and Mary and the little wee Son
Came to rest when the day was done;
And the little Child slept on his Mother's knee
In the shelter sweet of the juniper tree.

EILEEN DUGGAN

I Saw a Stable

I saw a stable, low and very bare,
A little child in a manger.
The oxen knew Him, had Him in their care,
To men He was a stranger.
The safety of the world was lying there,
And the world's danger.

MARY ELIZABETH COLERIDGE

Long, Long Ago

Winds through the olive trees
    Softly did blow,
Round little Bethlehem
    Long, long ago.

Sheep on the hillside lay
    Whiter than snow;
Shepherds were watching them,
    Long, long ago.

Then from the happy sky,
    Angels bent low,
Singing their songs of joy,
    Long, long ago.

For in a manger bed,
    Cradled we know,
Christ came to Bethlehem,
    Long, long ago.

ANONYMOUS

The Barn

"I am tired of this barn," said the colt,
    "And every day it snows.
Outside, there's no grass any more
    And icicles grow on my nose.
I am tired of hearing the cows
    Breathing and talking together,
I'm sick of the clucking of hens,
    I hate stables and winter weather."

"Hush! little colt," said the mare,
    "And a story I will tell
Of a barn like this one of ours
    And the things that there befell.
It was weather much like this
    And the beasts stood as we stand now
In the warm, good dark of the barn—
    A horse and an ass and a cow."

"And sheep?" asked the colt. "Yes, sheep,
    And a pig and a goat and a hen.
All of the beasts of the barnyard,
    The usual servants of men.
And into their midst came a Lady,
    And she was as cold as death,
But the animals leaned above her
    And made her warm with their breath.

"There was her Baby born
    And laid to sleep in the hay,
While music flooded the rafters
    And the barn was as light as day,
And angels and kings and shepherds
    Came to worship the Babe from afar,
But we looked at Him first of all creatures
    By the bright, strange light of a star!"

ELIZABETH COATSWORTH

Christmas Morning

If Bethlehem were here today,
Or this were very long ago,
There wouldn't be a winter time
Nor any cold or snow.

I'd run out through the garden gate,
And down along the pasture walk;
And off beside the cattle barns
I'd hear a kind of gentle talk.

I'd move the heavy iron chain
And pull away the wooden pin;
I'd push the door a little bit
And tiptoe very softly in.

The pigeons and the yellow hens
And all the cows would stand away;
Their eyes would open wide to see
A lady in the manger hay.

If this were very long ago
And Bethlehem were here today.

And Mother held my hand and smiled—
I mean the lady would—and she
Would take the woolly blankets off
Her little boy so I could see.

His shut-up eyes would be asleep,
And he would look like our John,
And he would be all crumpled too,
And have a pinkish color on.

I'd watch his breath go in and out.
His little clothes would all be white.
I'd slip my finger in his hand
To feel how he could hold it tight.

And she would smile and say, "Take care,"
The mother, Mary, would, "Take care;"
And I would kiss his little hand
And touch his hair.

While Mary put the blankets back
The gentle talk would soon begin.
And when I'd tiptoe softly out
I'd meet the wise men going in.

ELIZABETH MADOX ROBERTS

41

Marjorie's Almanac

Robins in the tree-top,
  Blossoms in the grass,
Green things a-growing
  Everywhere you pass;
Sudden little breezes,
  Showers of silver dew,
Black bough and bent twig
  Budding out anew,—
Don't you think that May-time's
  Pleasanter than March?

Apples in the orchard
  Mellowing one by one;
Strawberries upturning
  Soft cheeks to the sun;
Roses faint with sweetness,
  Lilies fair of face,
Drowsy scents and murmurs
  Haunting every place;
Lengths of golden sunshine,
  Moonlight bright as day,—
Don't you think that summer's
  Pleasanter than May?

Roger in the corn-patch
  Whistling Negro songs;
Pussy by the hearth-side
  Romping with the tongs;
Chestnuts in the ashes
  Bursting through the rind;
Red leaf and gold leaf
  Rustling down the wind;
Mother "doin' peaches"
  All the afternoon,—
Don't you think that autumn's
  Pleasanter than June?

Little fairy snow-flakes
  Dancing in the flue;
Old Mr. Santaclaus,
  What is keeping you?
Twilight and firelight
  Shadows come and go;
Merry chime of sleigh-bells
  Tinkling through the snow;
Mother knitting stockings
  (Pussy's got the ball),—
Don't you think that winter's
  Pleasanter than all?

THOMAS BAILEY ALDRICH

DOWN OUR STREET

Welcome

Little new neighbor, have you come to be
A playmate of mine from over the sea?
I'm glad you are here. Oh, won't it be fine
To learn all your games, and I'll teach you
      mine!
We won't understand all the words that we say,
But I'm sure that we both will know how to
      play.
So will you come now and swing while I swing,
And we'll sing all the songs that we love to sing.

ROSE WALDO

The Child Next Door

The child next door has a wreath on her hat;
Her afternoon frock sticks out like that,
   All soft and frilly;
She doesn't believe in fairies at all
(She told me over the garden wall)—
   She thinks they're silly.

The child next door has a watch of her own;
She has shiny hair and her name is Joan;
   (Mine's only Mary)—
But doesn't it seem very sad to you
To think that she never her whole life through
   Has seen a fairy?

ROSE FYLEMAN

"One, Two, Three!"

It was an old, old, old, old lady,
   And a boy that was half-past three;
And the way that they played together
   Was beautiful to see.

She couldn't go romping and jumping,
   And the boy no more could he;
For he was a thin little fellow,
   With a thin little twisted knee.

They sat in the yellow sunlight,
   Out under the maple tree;
And the game they played I'll tell you
   Just as it was told to me.

It was hide-and-go-seek they were playing,
   Though you'd never have known it to be—
With an old, old, old, old lady,
   And a boy with a twisted knee.

The boy would bend his face down
   On his little sound right knee,
And he guessed where she was hiding
   In guesses One, Two, Three.

"You are in the china closet!"
   He would laugh and cry with glee—
It wasn't the china closet,
   But he still had Two and Three.

"You are up in Papa's big bedroom,
   In the chest with the queer old key!"
And she said "You are *warm* and *warmer*;
   But you're not quite right," said she.

"It can't be the little cupboard
   Where Mamma's things used to be—
So it must be in the clothespress, Gran'ma!"
   And he found her with his Three.

Then she covered her face with her fingers,
   That were wrinkled and white and wee,
And she guessed where the boy was hiding,
   With a One and a Two and a Three.

And they never had stirred from their places
   Right under the maple tree—
This old, old, old, old lady,
   And the boy with the lame little knee—
This dear, dear, dear old lady,
   And the boy who was half-past three.

HENRY CUYLER BUNNER

Martha

"Once . . . once upon a time . . ."
Over and over again,
Martha would tell us her stories,
In the hazel glen.

Hers were those clear gray eyes
You watch, and the story seems
Told by their beautifulness
Tranquil as dreams.

She would sit with her two slim hands
Clasped round her bended knees;
While we on our elbows lolled,
And stared at ease.

Her voice and her narrow chin,
Her grave small lovely head,
Seemed half the meaning
Of the words she said.

"Once . . . once upon a time . . ."
Like a dream you dream in the night,
Fairies and gnomes stole out
In the leaf-green light.

And her beauty far away
Would fade, as her voice went on,
Till hazel and summer sun
And all were gone;—

All fordone and forgot;
And like the clouds in the height of the sky,
Our hearts stood still in the hush
Of an age gone by.

WALTER DE LA MARE

"Popcorn! Popcorn! Five a sack!"
And the children gather round
When they hear the whistle sound,
Staring wide-eyed, wonder-bound,
At the fragrant, snowy mound
　　Heaped inside the little window.
They watch his kindly face,
　　With his twinkly eyes of black;
They watch his mittened hands
　　As he deftly fills each sack.

Oh, I hear his whistle blowing
As through the streets I'm going.
　　"Popcorn! Popcorn! Five a sack!"
And I wish I were a child again,
With the years turned back!

EDITH OSBORNE

Barber's Clippers

The barber snips and snips
My hair with his scissors
And then he zips on
His clippers.
　　It clips
　　Up and down
　　And around
　　My hair in back.

　　　　Ssss ssss
　　　　It swishes
　　　　On the sides
　　　　Behind my ears.

　　　　Ssss ssss
　　　　It tickles
　　　　As it slides
　　　　　　Straight up the middle
　　　　　　Of my neck.

DOROTHY BARUCH

The Popcorn Man

Do you hear his whistle blowing—
　　Softly blowing as he stands
At the cold and wintry corner,
　　With mittens on his hands?

"Popcorn! Popcorn! Five a sack!"
And inside the little wagon,
Through the little steamy window,
You can see the white grains popping
　　And hopping round,
Hear a little, crisp staccato
　　Sort of sound,
Watch the fleecy grains go hopping,
　　Gaily dancing,
Softly dropping,
Never faltering or stopping,
　　Like a fall of fairy snow.

The Shoemaker

As I was a-walking the other day,
  I peeped in a window just over the way,
And old and bent and feeble too,
  There sat an old cobbler a-making a shoe.
With a rack-a-tac-tac and a rack-a-tac-too,
  This is the way he makes a shoe.
With a bright little awl he makes a hole,
  Right through the upper, and then through
    the sole
He puts in a peg, he puts in two,
  And a ha-ha-ha-ha and he hammers it
    through.

                              UNKNOWN

The Cobbler

Crooked heels
  And scuffy toes
Are all the kinds
  Of shoes he knows.

He patches up
  The broken places,
Sews the seams
  And shines their faces.

                    ELEANOR A. CHAFFEE

Indian Children

Where we walk to school each day
Indian children used to play—
All about our native land,
Where the shops and houses stand.

And the trees were very tall,
And there were no streets at all,
Not a church and not a steeple—
Only woods and Indian people.

Only wigwams on the ground,
And at night bears prowling round—
What a different place to-day
Where we live and work and play!

                    ANNETTE WYNNE

Portrait by a Neighbor

Before she has her floor swept
  Or her dishes done,
Any day you'll find her
  A-sunning in the sun!

It's long after midnight
  Her key's in the lock,
And you never see her chimney smoke
  Till past ten o'clock!

She digs in her garden
  With a shovel and a spoon,
She weeds her lazy lettuce
  By the light of the moon,

She walks up the walk
  Like a woman in a dream,
She forgets she borrowed butter
  And pays you back cream!

Her lawn looks like a meadow,
  And if she mows the place
She leaves the clover standing
  And the Queen Anne's lace!

                    EDNA ST. VINCENT MILLAY

The Circus Parade

Tomorrow, tomorrow's the circus parade!
Just think what I shall see!
What crowds of people in gay colored clothes
All lined up the street there will be.

And some of the children will have red
    balloons,
As up by the curbing they stand,
Then off in the distance we'll suddenly hear
The circus's big brass band!

Behind the crash bang! of the music they play,
Come riders in red velvet gowns,
And after them doing the funniest things,
A silly procession of clowns.

Then lions and tigers that pace up and down,
In wagons all painted with gold,
And monkeys a-playing just all kinds of tricks,
As they grimace and chatter and scold.

Oh, next there come camels and elephants, too,
With men on their backs astride,
And queer little ponies, no bigger than dogs,
And a donkey perhaps beside!

And then there come chariots rumbling by
With horses all four in a row;
And the wheezing, old calliope is
The very tail end of the show!

OLIVE BEAUPRE MILLER

48

Circus Parade

Here it comes! Here it comes!
I can hear the music playing;
I can hear the beating drums.

On parade! On parade!
Gaily plumed a horse and rider
Lead the circus cavalcade.

Knights in armor with their banners
Calmly riding by;
Horses hung with velvet trappings,
Stepping proudly high;
Circus wagons slowly clanking,
Drawn by six horse teams,
Red and gold and set with mirrors
Where the sunlight gleams;
Yawning lions in their cages;

Polar bear with swinging head;
Restless tiger pacing pacing
Back and forth with noiseless tread;
Horses snorting and cavorting
With wild yelling cowboy bands;
Dressed-up monkeys riding ponies,
Bowing as we clap our hands;
Herds of elephants and camels,
Marching one by one;
Troops of painted clowns advancing,
Playing tricks, and making fun.

At the end the steam calliope
Comes playing all too soon,
Saying the parade is over
As it pipes its wildest tune.

JAMES S. TIPPETT

49

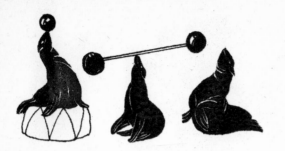

The Seals

The seals all flap
Their shining flips
And bounce balls on
Their nosey tips,
And beat a drum,
And catch a bar,
And wriggle with
How pleased they are.

DOROTHY ALDIS

Holding Hands

Elephants walking
Along the trails

Are holding hands
By holding tails.

Trunks and tails
Are handy things

When elephants walk
In Circus rings.

Elephants work
And elephants play

And elephants walk
And feel so gay.

And when they walk—
It never fails

They're holding hands
By holding tails.

LENORE M. LINK

Circus

The brass band blares,
The naphtha flares,
The sawdust smells,
Showmen ring bells,
And oh! right into the circus-ring
Comes such a lovely, lovely thing,
A milk-white pony with flying tress,
And a beautiful lady,
A beautiful lady,
A *beautiful* lady in a pink dress!
The red-and-white clown
For joy tumbles down,
Like a pink rose
Round she goes
On her tip-toes
With the pony under—
And then, oh, wonder!
The pony his milk-white tresses droops,
And the beautiful lady,
The *beautiful* lady,
Flies like a bird through the paper hoops!
The red-and-white clown for joy falls dead.
Then he waggles his feet and stands on his
    head.
And the little boys on the twopenny seats
Scream with laughter and suck their sweets.

ELEANOR FARJEON

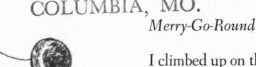

Our Circus

We had a circus in our shed
(Admission, three new pins a head).
And every girl and boy I know
Is talking yet about our show

They laughed so hard at Fatty Brown
When he came out to be the clown,
That all the neighbors ran to see
Whatever such a noise could be.

Our tin-pan and mouth-organ band
Played tunes that sounded simply grand;
We had a truly sawdust ring,
Pink lemonade, 'n everything.

The big menagerie was nice:
Three cats, one dog, and five white mice,
A parrot that Bill's uncle lent;
All underneath a bedspread tent.

Then Ned and Buster took a sheet
That covered them from head to feet
And made a horse that kicked and pranced
And when it heard the band, it danced.

And Sally Ann was "Bareback Queen!"
No finer rider could be seen;
She stood right up, and looked so proud,
But kissed her hand to all the crowd.

We took some chalk—blue, green, and red—
And made a "Tattooed Man" of Fred;
Jim juggled lighted cigarettes,
And Tom turned double somersets.

We had tall stilts—and flying rings—
And lots and lots of other things—
And every boy and girl I know
Said yes, it was a *dandy* show!

LAURA LEE RANDALL

Merry-Go-Round

I climbed up on the merry-go-round,
And it went round and round.

I climbed up on a big brown horse
And it went up and down.

    Around and round
    And up and down,
    Around and round
    And up and down.
    I sat high up
    On a big brown horse
    And rode around
    On the merry-go-round
    And rode around

On the merry-go-round
I rode around
    On the merry-go-round
      Around
        And round
        And
          Round.

DOROTHY W. BARUCH

At the Theater

The sun was bright when we went in,
 But night and lights were there,
The walls had golden trimming on
 And plush on every chair.

The people talked; the music played,
 Then it grew black as pitch,
Yes, black as closets full of clothes,
 Or caves, I don't know which.

The curtain rolled itself away,
 It went I don't know where,
But, oh, that country just beyond,
 I do wish we lived there!

The mountain peaks more jagged rise,
 Grass grows more green than here;
The people there have redder cheeks,
 And clothes more gay and queer.

They laugh and smile, but not the same,
 Exactly as we do,
And if they ever have to cry
 Their tears are different, too—

More shiny, somehow, and more sad,
 You hold your breath to see
If everything will come out right
 And they'll live happily;

If Pierrot will kiss Pierrette
 Beneath an orange moon,
And Harlequin and Columbine
Outwit old Pantaloon.

You know they will, they always do,
 But still your heart must beat,
And you must pray they will be saved,
 And tremble in your seat.

And then it's over and they bow
 All edged about with light,
The curtain rattles down and shuts
 Them every one from sight.

It's strange to find the afternoon
 Still bright outside the door,
And all the people hurrying by
 The way they were before!

RACHEL FIELD

Shop Windows

Mother likes the frocks and hats
And pretty stuffs and coloured mats.

Daddy never, never looks
At anything but pipes and books.

Auntie's fond of chains and rings
And all the sparkly diamond things.

Richard likes machines the best;
He doesn't care about the rest.

Nannie always loves to stop
In front of every single shop.

But I don't want to wait for a minute
Till we get to the one with the puppy dogs in it.

ROSE FYLEMAN

"To Think!"

To think I once saw grocery shops
    With but a casual eye
And fingered figs and apricots
    As one who came to buy.

To think I never dreamed of how
    Bananas sway in rain
And often looked at oranges
    Yet never thought of Spain.

And in those wasted days I saw
    No sails above the tea
For grocery shops were grocery shops
    Not hemispheres to me.

ELIZABETH COATSWORTH

Jim at the Corner

Jim was a Sailor
Who sailed on the sea.
Now he sits at the corner
From breakfast to tea,
With a nod and a twinkle
For you and for me.

His hair is quite silver,
His eyes are quite blue,
His legs have got pains
So he's nothing to do
But to nod and to twinkle
At me and at you.

He tells all the weather
Without any fuss,
When he says it is thus
Then of *course* it is thus,
He nods as he says it
And twinkles at us.

He knows the world over
From east to west rim,
Now he sits on his box
And the whole world knows Jim.
He nods to the world,
And the world nods to him.

ELEANOR FARJEON

A Piper

A piper in the streets today
Set up, and tuned, and started to play,
And away, away, away on the tide
On the tide of his music we started; on
        every side
Door and windows were opened wide,
And men left down their work and came,
And women with petticoats colored like flame.
And little bare feet that were blue with cold,
Went dancing back to the age of gold,
And all the world went gay, went gay,
For half an hour in the street today.

SEUMAS O'SULLIVAN

The House With Nobody In It

Whenever I walk to Suffern along the Erie
  track
I go by a poor old farmhouse with its shingles
  broken and black.
I suppose I've passed it a hundred times, but I
  always stop for a minute
And look at the house, the tragic house, the
  house with nobody in it.

I never have seen a haunted house, but I hear
  there are such things;
That they hold the talk of spirits, their mirth
  and sorrowings.
I know this house isn't haunted, and I wish it
  were, I do;
For it wouldn't be so lonely if it had a ghost or
  two.

This house on the road to Suffern needs a
  dozen panes of glass,
And somebody ought to weed the walk and
  take a scythe to the grass.
It needs new paint and shingles, and the vines
  should be trimmed and tied;
But what it needs the most of all is some people
  living inside.

If I had a lot of money and all my debts were
  paid
I'd put a gang of men to work with brush and
  saw and spade.
I'd buy that place and fix it up the way it used
  to be
And I'd find some people who wanted a home
  and give it to them free.

Now, a new house standing empty, with
  staring window and door,
Looks idle, perhaps, and foolish, like a hat on
  its block in the store.
But there's nothing mournful about it; it
  cannot be sad and lone
For the lack of something within it that it has
  never known.

But a house that has done what a house should
  do, a house that has sheltered life,
That has put its loving wooden arms around a
  man and his wife,
A house that has echoed a baby's laugh and
  held up his stumbling feet,
Is the saddest sight, when it's left alone, that
  ever your eyes could meet.

So whenever I go to Suffern along the Erie
  track
I never go by the empty house without
  stopping and looking back,
Yet it hurts me to look at the crumbling roof
  and the shutters fallen apart,
For I can't help thinking the poor old house is
  a house with a broken heart.

JOYCE KILMER

ALL OUT OF DOORS

Child's Song

I have a garden of my own,
  Shining with flow'rs of ev'ry hue;
I loved it dearly while alone,
  But I shall love it more with you:
And there the golden bees shall come,
  In summer-time at break of morn,
And wake us with their busy hum
  Around the Siha's fragrant thorn.

I have a fawn from Aden's land,
  On leafy buds and berries nurst,
And you shall feed him from your hand,
  Though he may start with fear at first.
And I will lead you where he lies
  For shelter in the noontide heat;
And you may touch his sleeping eyes,
  And feel his little silv'ry feet.

THOMAS MOORE

Foolish Flowers

We've Foxgloves in our garden;
  How careless they must be
To leave their gloves out hanging
  Where everyone can see!

And Bachelors leave their Buttons
  In the same careless way,
If I should do the same with mine,
  What would my mother say?

We've lots of Larkspurs in the Yard—
  Larks only fly and sing—
Birds surely don't need spurs because
  They don't ride anything!

And as for Johnny-Jump-Ups—
  I saw a hornet light
On one of them the other day,
  He didn't jump a mite!

RUPERT SARGENT HOLLAND

A Hint to the Wise

I know a little garden path
 That leads you through the trees,
Past flower-beds and hollyhocks
 And by the homes of bees,
Until at last it brings you to
 A little fountain bath
Where tiny birds may wash themselves.
 If you go down that path,
Remember to be careful what
 You say. A little bird
May cause a lot of trouble by
 Repeating what he's heard.

PRINGLE BARRET

A Tea-Party

You see, merry Phillis, that dear little maid,
 Has invited Belinda to tea;
Her nice little garden is shaded by trees,—
 What pleasanter place could there be?

There's a cake full of plums, there are
 strawberries too,
 And the table is set on the green;
I'm fond of a carpet all daisies and grass,—
 Could a prettier picture be seen?

A blackbird (yes, blackbirds delight in warm
 weather),
 Is flitting from yonder high spray;
He sees the two little ones talking together,—
 No wonder the blackbird is gay.

KATE GREENAWAY

Baby Seeds

In a milkweed cradle,
 Snug and warm,
Baby seeds are hiding,
 Safe from harm.
Open wide the cradle,
 Hold it high!
Come, Mr. Wind,
 Help them fly.

UNKNOWN

How the Flowers Grow

This is how the flowers grow:
I have watched them and I know.

First, above the ground is seen
A tiny blade of purest green,
Reaching up and peeping forth
East and west and south and north.

Then it shoots up day by day,
Circling in a curious way
Round a blossom, which it keeps
Warm and cozy while it sleeps.

Then the sunbeams find their way
To the sleeping bud and say,
"We are children of the sun
Sent to wake thee, little one."

And the leaflet opening wide
Shows the tiny bud inside,
Peeping with half-opened eye
On the bright and sunny sky.

Breezes from the west and south
Lay their kisses on its mouth;
Till the petals all are grown,
And the bud's a flower blown.

This is how the flowers grow:
I have watched them and I know.

GABRIEL SETOUN

57

The Violet

A violet by a mossy stone,
Half hidden from the eye,
Fair as a star, when only one
Is shining in the sky.

WILLIAM WORDSWORTH

Daffodils

In spite of cold and chills
That usher in the early spring,
We have the daffodils.

JAPANESE HOKKU

Iris

Ere yet the sun is high,
All blue the iris blossoms wave,
The color of the sky.

UNKNOWN (Japanese)

Crocuses

The sunrise tints the dew,
The yellow crocuses are out,
And I must pick a few.

UNKNOWN (Japanese)

Dandelion

There was a pretty dandelion
With lovely, fluffy hair,
That glistened in the sunshine
And in the summer air.
But oh! this pretty dandelion
Soon grew old and grey;
And, sad to tell! her charming hair
Blew many miles away.

UNKNOWN

Golden Tacks

Miss April's come and I have found
She's spread a carpet on the ground.
It's the nicest rug I've ever seen,
So big and soft and bright and green.
It hides the Earth's old dirty brown
And all the ugly-wrinkly cracks—
It can't blow off, it's fastened down
With golden dandelion tacks!

MILDRED D. SHACKLETT

Her Choice

If I could not be the girl I am
With milk for tea, and bread and jam,
A bed to sleep in, warm and dry,
Not wet with dew, where crickets cry—
If I had to be a flower, I think
I'd love to be a rose—and pink!

MATTIE LEE HAUSGEN

The Little Rose Tree

Every rose on the little tree
Is making a different face at me!

Some look surprised when I pass by,
And others droop—but they are shy.

These two whose heads together press
Tell secrets I could never guess.

Some have their heads thrown back to sing,
And all the buds are listening.

I wonder if the gardener knows,
Or if he calls each just a rose?

RACHEL FIELD

Lilies

I thought I saw white clouds, but no!—
    Bending across the fence,
    White lilies in a row!

SHIKO 1665-1731

Lilies of the Valley

Down in the grassy lowland dells,
They softly swing—white lily bells;
A pale green stem upon which grows
Fair white-frilled cups in tiny rows.
Each wee flower has a heart of gold,
Each cup a drop of dew would hold;
And by their fragrance you may know
Where lilies of the valley grow.

MARION MITCHELL WALKER

Little White Lily

Little White Lily sat by a stone,
Drooping and waiting till the sun shone.
Little White Lily sunshine has fed;
Little White Lily is lifting her head.

Little White Lily said: "It is good,
Little White Lily's clothing and food."
Little White Lily dressed like a bride!
Shining with whiteness, and crowned beside!

Little White Lily drooping with pain,
Waiting and waiting for the wet rain,
Little White Lily holdeth her cup;
Rain is fast falling and filling it up.

Little White Lily said: "Good again,
When I am thirsty to have the nice rain.
Now I am stronger, now I am cool;
Heat cannot burn me, my veins are so full."

Little White Lily smells very sweet;
On her head sunshine, rain at her feet.
Thanks to the sunshine, thanks to the rain,
Little White Lily is happy again.

GEORGE MACDONALD

Jack-in-the-Pulpit

Four of us went to the woods one day,
Keeping the trail in the Indian way,
    Creeping, crawling,
    Sometimes sprawling,
Pushing through the bushes; and there we
        found
A little green pulpit stuck in the ground
And in the pulpit a brown man stood,
Preaching to all the folk in the wood.

We lay as quiet as Indians do,
Because each one of the four of us knew,
    At any sound,
    The creatures 'round,
The squirrels and chipmunks, the birds and
        bees,
Would fly away through the ring of trees,
And Jack-in-the-Pulpit would stop his speech
If he knew we four were in easy reach.

We listened as hard as ever we could,
But not a one of us understood,
    Or even heard,
    A single word,
Though I saw a chipmunk nod his head
As if he knew what the preacher said,
And a big gray squirrel clapped his paws
When he thought it was time for applause.

Many and many a Jack we've found,
But none of us ever heard a sound;
    So I suppose
    That Jackie knows
When children try to hear him preach,
And talks in some peculiar speech;
I wonder if we could find a way
To hear what Jacks-in-the-Pulpits say?

RUPERT SARGENT HOLLAND

Apple Blossom

Lady Apple Blossom
   Just arrived in town,
Wears a light green bonnet
   And a snowy gown.

The pretty dress is—
   What do you think?
Five white petals
   Just touched with pink.

KATE L. BROWN

The Faithless Flowers

I went this morning down to where the
   Johnny-Jump-Ups grow
Like naughty purple faces nodding in a row.
I stayed 'most all the morning there—I sat down
   on a stump
And watched and watched and watched
   them—and they never gave a jump!

And Golden Glow that stands up tall and
   yellow by the fence,
It doesn't glow a single bit—it's only just
   pretense—
I ran down after tea last night to watch them
   in the dark—
I had to light a match to see; they didn't give a
   spark!

And then the Bouncing Bets don't bounce—I
   tried them yesterday,
I picked up a big pink bunch down in the
   meadow where they stay,
I took a piece of string I had and tied them in
   a ball,
And threw them down as hard as hard—they
   never bounced at all!

And Tiger Lilies may look fierce, to meet them
   all alone,
All tall and black and yellowy and nodding by
   a stone,

But they're no more like tigers than the dogwood's like a dog,
Or bulrushes are like a bull or toadwort like a
   frog!

I like the flowers very much—they're pleasant
   as can be
For bunches on the table, and to pick and wear
   and see,
But still it doesn't seem quite fair—it does seem
   very queer—
They don't do what they're named for—not at
   any time of year!

MARGARET WIDDEMER

Plum Blossoms

   Far across hill and dale
The blossoms of the plum have cast
   A delicate pink veil.

BASHO

   So sweet the plum trees smell!
Would that the brush that paints the flower
   Could paint the scent as well.

JAPANESE HOKKU

   I came to look, and lo,
The plum tree petals scatter down
   A fall of purest snow.

REINKO 1728-99

Poplars

The poplar is a lonely tree;
It has no branches spreading wide
Where birds may sing or squirrels hide.
It throws no shadow on the grass
Tempting the wayfarers who pass
To stop and sit there quietly.

The poplar is a slender tree;
It has no boughs where children try
To climb far off into the sky.
To hold a swing, it's far too weak,
Too small it is for hide-and-seek;
Friendless, forsaken it must be.

The poplar is a restless tree;
At every breeze its branches bend
And signal to the child, "Come, friend;"
Its leaves forever whispering
To thrush and robin, "Stay and sing."
They pass. It quivers plaintively.

Poplars are lonely. They must grow
Close to each other in a row.

EDWARD BLISS REED

And just as quick
    They drop away.
I wish the apple
    Trees would stay
In bloom at least
    A week or two;
But that is not
    The way they do.

Almost at once
    The petals fall
Down on the grass
    And garden wall.
They go adrift
    On every breeze
Like snowflakes off
    The apple trees.

It is the oddest
    Thing to see:
The lawn as green
    As green can be,
And then the orchard
    Where each row
Of apple trees
    Stands in the snow.

RALPH BERGENGREN

Apple Blossoms

There is a day
    That comes in spring
When apples trees
    Are blossoming.
They blossom out
    So quick some morn
It's like a giant
    Popping corn.

And from my window
    I can smell
The apple blossoms
    Very well.

Birch Trees

The night is white,
    The moon is high,
The birch trees lean
    Against the sky.

The cruel winds
    Have blown away
Each little leaf
    Of silver gray.

O lonely trees
    As white as wool . . .
That moonlight makes
    So beautiful.

JOHN RICHARD MORELAND

The All Alone Tree

There's a tree that is growing alone on the hill,
By the path that winds up at the back of the
    mill,
And we're awfully fond of it, Maudie and me,
And we call it the All Alone, All Alone Tree.

It is old, and it's wrinkled and twisted and dry,
And it grows by itself with no other tree nigh,
And we always sit under it, Maudie and me,
Because it's the All Alone, All Alone Tree.

In the bright summer-time when they're
    cutting the hay,
Then the birds come and sing in its branches
    all day,
And we're awfully glad of this, Maudie and
    me,
Because it's the All Alone, All Alone Tree.

But in the dark winter the birds have all flown,
And we know that it's standing there, quite,
    quite alone,
So we creep out and kiss it then, Maudie and
    me,
Because it's the All Alone, All Alone Tree.

F. O'NEIL GALLAGHER

The Tree

The tree's early leaf buds were bursting their
    brown:
"Shall I take them away?" said the frost,
    sweeping down.
    "No, dear; leave them alone
    Till blossoms here have grown,"
Prayed the tree, while it trembled from rootlet
    to crown.

The tree bore its blossoms, and all the birds
    sung:
"Shall I take them away?" said the wind, as it
    swung.
    "No, dear; leave them alone
    Till berries here have grown,"
Said the tree, while its leaflets quivering hung.

The tree bore its fruit in the midsummer glow:
Said the girl, "May I gather thy berries or no?"
    "Yes, dear, all thou canst see;
    Take them; all are for thee,"
Said the tree, while it bent its laden boughs low.

BJORNSTJERNE BJORNSON

Pussy Willows

I came on them yesterday (merely by chance),
Those newly born pussies, asleep on a branch;
Each curled up so tight in a fluff of a ball
That I could not see ear-points or tail-tips at all;
But I thought that I heard, when the March
    wind was stirring,

A soft little sound like the note of purring.
I wonder if they would have leaped from their
    bough
And arched their wee backs with a frightened
    "Meow!"
If I dared to tell them in one warning cry
That a fierce patch of dogwood was growing
    close by.

ROWENA BASTIN BENNETT

Pussy Willows

I have some dainty pussies here
    All dressed in soft gray fur,
But you might listen all day long
    And not once hear them purr.

Nor do they run and frisk about,—
    These pretty living things,
But closely round a slender twig
    Each tiny pussy clings.

All through the winter's storms and cold,
    These furry babies swung,
In cradle beds of shining brown,
    On willow branches hung.

The rough winds sang their lullaby
    And rocked them to and fro,
And all about their sleepy heads
    Drifted the cold white snow.

But by and by the sunbeams warm
    Peeped into each small bed,
And said: "Come, Pussies, waken now,
    For winter days are fled."

So bravely come the Pussies forth,
    Though still the cold wind blows,
And up and down the long, brown stems
    They cling in shining rows.

But when the days grow long and bright,
    And breezes not so cold,
They'll change their dress of silver fur
    For robes of green and gold.

                       MARY E. PLUMMER

Hail on the Pine Trees

    The hail falls pitterpat,
And fiercely rattles down upon
    The brave old pine tree's hat.

               BASHO

The Willows

By the little river,
    Still and deep and brown,
Grow the graceful willows,
    Gently dipping down.

Dipping down and brushing
    Everything that floats—
Leaves and logs and fishes,
    And the passing boats.

Were they water maidens
    In the long ago,
That they lean out sadly
    Looking down below?

In the misty twilight
    You can see their hair,
Weeping water maidens
    That were once so fair.

               WALTER PRICHARD EATON

Little Rain

When I was making myself a game
Up in the garden, a little rain came.

It fell down quick in a sort of rush,
And I crawled back under the snowball bush.

I could hear the big drops hit the ground
And see little puddles of dust fly round.

A chicken came till the rain was gone;
He had just a very few feathers on.

He shivered a little under his skin,
And then he shut his eyeballs in.

Even after the rain had begun to hush
It kept on raining up in the bush.

One big flat drop came sliding down,
And a ladybug that was red and brown

Was up on a little stem waiting there,
And I got some rain in my hair.

ELIZABETH MADOX ROBERTS

The Leaves Drink

Whenever the rain comes gently down,
    It gurgles as it's sinking
Into the ground so low—
    I know the leaves are drinking.

ALICE WILKINS

Vegetables

A carrot has a green fringed top;
    A beet is royal red;
And lettuces are curious,
    All curled and run to head.

Some beans have strings to tie them on,
    And, what is still more queer,
Ripe corn is nothing more or less
    Than one enormous ear!

But when potatoes all have eyes,
    Why is it they should be
Put in the ground and covered up—
    Where it's too dark to see?

RACHEL FIELD

The Green Grass Growing All Around

There was a tree stood in the ground,
The prettiest tree you ever did see;
The tree in the wood, and the wood in the
  ground,
And the green grass growing all around.
And the green grass growing all around.

And on this tree there was a limb,
The prettiest limb you ever did see;
The limb on the tree, and the tree in the wood,
The tree in the wood, and the wood in the
  ground,
And the green grass growing all around.
And the green grass growing all around.

And on this limb there was a bough,
The prettiest bough you ever did see;
The bough on the limb, and the limb on the
  tree,
The limb on the tree, and the tree in the wood,
The tree in the wood, and the wood in the
  ground,
And the green grass growing all around.
And the green grass growing all around.

Now on this bough there was a nest,
The prettiest nest you ever did see;
The nest on the bough, and the bough on the
  limb,
The bough on the limb, and the limb on the
  tree,
The limb on the tree, and the tree in the wood,
The tree in the wood, and the wood in the
  ground,
And the green grass growing all around.
And the green grass growing all around.

And in the nest there were some eggs,
The prettiest eggs you ever did see;
Eggs in the nest, and the nest on the bough,
The nest on the bough, and the bough on the
  limb,
The bough on the limb, and the limb on the
  tree,
The limb on the tree, and the tree in the wood,
The tree in the wood, and the wood in the
  ground,
And the green grass growing all around.
And the green grass growing all around.

FOLK RHYME

CREATURES, BIG AND SMALL

Familiar Friends

The horses, the pigs,
And the chickens,
The turkeys, the ducks
And the sheep!
I can see all my friends
From my window
As soon as I waken
From sleep.

The cat on the fence
Is out walking.
The geese have gone down
For a swim.
The pony comes trotting
Right up to the gate;
He knows I have candy
For him.

The cows in the pasture
Are switching
Their tails to keep off
The flies.
And the old mother dog
Has come out in the yard
With five pups to give me
A surprise.

JAMES S. TIPPETT

The Pasture

I'm going out to clean the pasture spring;
I'll only stop to rake the leaves away
(And wait to watch the water clear, I may):
I sha'n't be gone long. You come too.

I'm going out to fetch the little calf
That's standing by the mother. It's so young,
It totters when she licks it with her tongue.
I sha'n't be gone long. You come too.

ROBERT FROST

Cattle

How cool the cattle seem!
They love to swish their tails and stand
   Knee-deep within the stream.

BANKO

68

The Happy Sheep

All through the night the happy sheep
Lie in the meadow grass asleep.

Their wool keeps out the frost and rain
Until the sun comes round again.

They have no buttons to undo,
Nor hair to brush like me and you.

And with the light they lift their heads
To find their breakfast on their beds,

Or rise and walk about and eat
The carpet underneath their feet.

WILFRED THORLEY

The Escape

I'm not afraid of rats and mice
    (At least not much),
A spider I can look at twice
    (And even touch);
I do not mind the cows and sheep
That people in the country keep
(No matter how they turn and stare
I pass along and never care);
But once when I was out a-walking
A great gray goose came at me squawking;
He flew ni-nipping at my knee,
I was as scared as I could be
I shouldn't have escaped at all
Without my little parasol!

EMILY ROSE BURT

The Scarecrow

A scarecrow stood in a field one day,
    Stuffed with straw,
    Stuffed with hay;
He watched the folk on the king's highway,
    But never a word said he.

Much he saw but naught did heed,
    Knowing not night,
    Knowing not day,
For having naught did nothing heed
    And never a word said he.

A little grey mouse had made its nest,
    Oh so wee,
    Oh so grey,
In a sleeve of a coat that was poor Tom's best,
    But the scarecrow naught said he.

His hat was the home of a small jenny wren,
    Ever so sweet,
    Ever so gay,
A squirrel had put by his fear of men,
    And hissed him, but naught heeded he.

Ragged old man, I loved him well,
    Stuffed with straw,
    Stuffed with hay,
Many's the tale that he could tell,
    But never a word says he.

MICHAEL FRANKLIN

69

The Hairy Dog

My dog's so furry I've not seen
His face for years and years:
His eyes are buried out of sight,
I only guess his ears.

When people ask me for his breed,
I do not know or care:
He has the beauty of them all
Hidden beneath his hair.

HERBERT ASQUITH

My Dog

His nose is short and scrubby;
    His ears hang rather low;
And he always brings the stick back,
    No matter how far you throw.

He gets spanked rather often
    For things he shouldn't do,
Like lying-on-beds, and barking,
    And eating up shoes when they're new.

He always wants to be going
    Where he isn't supposed to go.
He tracks up the house when it's snowing—
    Oh, puppy, I love you so!

MARCHETTE GAYLORD CHUTE

Cat

My cat
Is quiet.
She moves without a sound.
Sometimes she stretches herself high and
        curving
On tiptoe.
Sometimes she crouches low
And creeping.

Sometimes she rubs herself against a chair,
And there
    With a *miew* and a *miew*
    And a purrrr purrrr purrrr
    She curls up
    And goes to sleep.

My cat
Lives through a black hole
Under the house.
So one day I
Crawled in after her.
And it was dark
And I sat
And didn't know
Where to go.
And then—
Two yellow-white
Round little lights
Came moving . . . moving . . . toward me.
And there
With a *miew* and a *miew*
And a purrrr purrrr purrrr
My cat
Rubbed, soft, against me.

    And I knew
    The lights
    Were MY CAT'S EYES
    In the dark.

DOROTHY BARUCH

70

Hearth

A cat sat quaintly by the fire
    And watched the burning coals
And watched the little flames aspire
    Like small decrepit souls.
Queer little fire with coals so fat
    And crooked flames that rise,
No queerer than the little cat
    With fire in its eyes.

PEGGY BACON

Song for a Child

My kitty has a little song
She hums inside of her;
She curls up by the kitchen fire
And then begins to purr.

It sounds just like she's winding up
A tiny clock she keeps
Inside her beautiful fur coat
To wake her, when she sleeps.

HELEN BAYLEY DAVIS

Cat

The black cat yawns
Opens her jaws,
Stretches her legs,
And shows her claws.

Then she gets up
And stands on four
Long stiff legs
And yawns some more.

She shows her sharp teeth,
She stretches her lip,
Her slice of a tongue
Turns up at the tip.

Lifting herself
On her delicate toes,
She arches her back
As high as it goes.

She lets herself down
With particular care,
And pads away
With her tail in the air.

MARY BRITTON MILLER

The Mouse

I heard a mouse
Bitterly complaining
In a crack of moonlight
Aslant on the floor—

"Little I ask
And that little is not granted.
There are few crumbs
In this world any more.

"The bread-box is tin
And I cannot get in.

"The jam's in a jar
My teeth cannot mar.

"The cheese sits by itself
On the pantry shelf—

"All night I run
Searching and seeking,
All night I run
About on the floor.

"Moonlight is there
And a bare place for dancing,
But no little feast
Is spread any more."

ELIZABETH COATSWORTH

The House of the Mouse

The house of the mouse
is a wee little house,
a green little house in the grass,
which big clumsy folk
may hunt and may poke
and still never see as they pass
this sweet little, neat little,
wee little, green little,
cuddle-down hide-away
house in the grass.

LUCY SPRAGUE MITCHELL

The Chickens

Said the first little chicken,
    With a queer little squirm,
"I wish I could find
    A fat little worm."

Said the next little chicken,
    With an odd little shrug,
"I wish I could find
    A fat little slug."

Said the third little chicken,
    With a sharp little squeal,
"I wish I could find
    Some nice yellow meal."

Said the fourth little chicken,
    With a small sigh of grief,
"I wish I could find
    A little green leaf."

Said the fifth little chicken,
    With a faint little moan,
"I wish I could find
    A wee gravel stone."

"Now, see here," said the mother,
    From the green garden patch,
"If you want any breakfast,
    Just come here and scratch."

UNKNOWN

Chanticleer

High and proud on the barnyard fence
Walks rooster in the morning.
He shakes his comb, he shakes his tail
And gives his daily warning.

"Get up, you lazy boys and girls,
It's time you should be dressing!"
I wonder if he keeps a clock,
Or if he's only guessing.

JOHN FARRAR

The Ducks

When our ducks waddle to the pond,
They're awkward as awkward can be—
But when they get in the water and swim,
They glide most gracefully.

ALICE WILKINS

Duck's Ditty

All along the backwater,
Through the rushes tall,
Ducks are a-dabbling,
Up tails all!

Ducks' tails, drakes' tails,
Yellow feet a-quiver,
Yellow bills all out of sight
Busy in the river!

Slushy green undergrowth
Where the roach swim—
Here we keep our larder,
Cool and full and dim!

Every one for what he likes!
We like to be
Heads down, tails up,
Dabbling free!

High in the blue above
Swifts whirl and call—
We are down a-dabbling
Up tails all!

KENNETH GRAHAME

Ducks at Dawn

"Quack! Quack!"
Said seven ducks at dawn
While night dew
Glimmered on the lawn.

"Quack! Quack!" they said.
"It's time to eat.
We'll go hunt mushrooms
For a treat."

And in the light
Of early dawn
I saw them chasing
On the lawn.

They sought their treat
With hungry quacks
And marked the dew
With criss-cross tracks.

They ate the mushrooms
One by one
And quacked to greet
The rising sun.

But in my bed
I settled back
And slept to tunes
Of "Quack! Quack! Quack!"

JAMES S. TIPPETT

The Wonderful Meadow

Over in the meadow, in the sand, in the sun,
Lived an old Mother-Toad and her little toady
one.
"Leap," said the mamma. "I'll leap," said
the one,
And she leaped with her mamma in the sand,
in the sun.

Over in the meadow, where the water runs
blue,
Lived an old Mother-Fish and her little fishes
two.
"Swim," said the mamma. "We'll swim," said
the two,
And they swam and they danced in the water
so blue.

Over in the meadow, in the old apple-tree,
Lived a Mother-Bluebird and her little birdies
three.
"Sing," said the mamma. "We'll sing," said the
three,
And they sang their sweet songs in the old
apple-tree.

Over in the meadow, in the reeds on the shore,
Lived a Mother-Muskrat and her little ratties
four.
"Dive," said the mamma. "We'll dive," said the
four.
And they dove every day, 'mid the reeds on the
shore.

Over in the meadow, in their snug little hive,
Lived a Mother-Honeybee, and the little bees
were five.
"Buzz," said the mamma. "We'll buzz," said
the five.
And they buzzed and made honey in their busy
little hive.

Over in the meadow, in a nest built of sticks,
Lived a black Mother-Crow and her little
blackies six.

"Caw," said the mamma. "We'll caw," said
the six,
And they cawed and they cawed in their nest
built of sticks.

Over in the meadow, in the calm summer even,
Lived a Mother-Firefly, and her little flies were
seven.
"Shine," said the mamma. "We'll shine," said
the seven,
And they shone like the stars, in the calm
summer even.

Over in the meadow, on an old mossy gate,
Lived a Mother-Lizard, and her little lizards
eight.
"Bask," said the mamma. "We'll bask," said the
eight,
And they basked in the sun on the old mossy
gate.

Over in the meadow, where the clear waters
shine,
Lived a Mother-Bullfrog, and her little froggies
nine.
"Croak," said the mamma. "We'll croak," said
the nine,
And they croaked every night where the clear
waters shine.

Over in the meadow, in her sly little den,
Lived a Mother-Spider, and her little spiders
ten.
"Spin," said the mamma. "We'll spin," said the
ten,
And they spun their lace webs in their little sly
den.

Over in the meadow, where the grass is soft and
even,
Lived a Mother-Cricket and her little ones
eleven.
"Chirp," said the mamma. "We'll chirp," said
the eleven,
And they chirped and they chirped where the
grass is soft and even.

Over in the meadow, where the men dig and
    delve,
Lived an old Mother-Ant and her little anties
    twelve.
"Toil," said the mamma. "We'll toil," said the
    twelve,
And they toiled every day when the men dig
    and delve.

OLIVE A. WADSWORTH

The Little Turtle

There was a little turtle.
He lived in a box.
He swam in a puddle.
He climbed on the rocks.

He snapped at a mosquito.
He snapped at a flea.
He snapped at a minnow.
And he snapped at me.

He caught the mosquito.
He caught the flea.
He caught the minnow.
But he didn't catch me.

VACHEL LINDSAY

Ways of Traveling

Little Mister Polliwog,
You swim to and fro.
When you turn into a frog
You'll hop where'er you go.

ALICE WILKINS

Twenty Froggies

Twenty froggies went to school
Down beside a rushy pool;
Twenty little coats of green,
Twenty vests all white and clean.

"We must be in time," said they.
"First we study, then we play;
That is how we keep the rule,
When we froggies go to school."

Master Bullfrog, grave and stern,
Called the classes in their turn;
Taught them how to nobly strive,
Likewise how to leap and dive.

From his seat upon a log,
Showed them how to say, "Ker-chog!"
Also how to dodge a blow
From the sticks that bad boys throw.

Twenty froggies grew up fast;
Bullfrogs they became at last.
Not one dunce was in the lot,
Not one lesson they forgot.

Polished in a high degree,
As each froggie ought to be,
Now they sit on other logs,
Teaching other little frogs.

GEORGE COOPER

A Friend in the Garden

He is not John the gardener,
  And yet the whole day long
Employs himself most usefully
  The flower-beds among.

He is not Tom the pussy-cat;
  And yet the other day,
With stealthy stride and glistening eye,
  He crept upon his prey.

He is not Dash, the dear old dog,
  And yet, perhaps, if you
Took pains with him and petted him,
  You'd come to love him too.

He's not a blackbird, though he chirps
  And though he once was black;
But now he wears a loose, grey coat,
  All wrinkled in the back.

He's got a very dirty face,
  And very shining eyes!
He sometimes comes and sits indoors;
  He looks — and p'raps is — wise.

But in a sunny flower-bed
  He has his fixed abode;
He eats the things that eat my plants—
  He is a friendly TOAD.

JULIANA HORATIA EWING

Little Snail

I saw a little snail
Come down the garden walk.
He wagged his head this way . . . that way . . .
Like a clown in a circus.
He looked from side to side
As though he were from a different country.
I have always said he carries his house on his
      back . . .
To-day in the rain
I saw that it was his umbrella!

HILDA CONKLING

76

A Garden Path

There is a little garden path
   (I play it is a street),
And you could never guess, I know,
When in it I a-walking go
   How many folks I meet

There's funny Mr. Hoppy Toad,
   Quite elderly and fat,
Who always winks and hurries by
And will not wait for me, though I
   Should like to have a chat.

And Mrs. Snail, who takes her house
   Wherever she must go;
I longed to get a peep inside,
But as the door's not very wide
   I couldn't quite, you know.

One day a whole procession passed,
   A lovely ant parade.
They went like soldiers marching by,
They seemed so orderly and spry
   And not a bit afraid.

I like the little garden path,
   And so, I'm sure, would you.
If you will go with me some day
I'll show you all along the way,
   And all the people too.

               MAY JUSTUS

The Snail

The snail he lives in his hard round house,
   In the orchard, under the tree:
Says he, "I have but a single room;
   But it's large enough for me."

The snail in his little house doth dwell
   All the week from end to end,
You're at home, Master Snail; that's all
     very well.
   But you never receive a friend.

               UNKNOWN

77

Hurt no living thing:
    Ladybird, nor butterfly,
Nor moth with dusty wing,
    Nor cricket chirping cheerily,
Nor grasshopper so light of leap,
    Nor dancing gnat, nor beetle fat,
Nor harmless worms that creep.

CHRISTINA ROSSETTI

A Lovely Bed

Each morning bees and butterflies
Have wiped the dewdrops from their eyes
And flown away on whirring wings
Before our bell for breakfast rings!
They sleep in hollyhocks so pink—
A soft and lovely bed I think!

MATTIE LEE HAUSGEN

Ke-Ni-Ga Song

(American Indian)

The poor little bee
That lives in the tree,
The poor little bee
That lives in the tree
Has only one arrow
In his quiver.

Trans. by NATALIE BARNES

Fuzzy Wuzzy, Creepy Crawly

Fuzzy wuzzy, creepy crawly
    Caterpillar funny,
You will be a butterfly
    When the days are sunny.

Winging, flinging, dancing, springing
    Butterfly so yellow,
You were once a caterpillar,
    Wiggly, wiggly fellow.

LILLIAN SCHULZ

The Tired Caterpillar

A tired caterpillar went to sleep one day
In a snug little cradle of silken gray.
And he said, as he softly curled up in his nest,
"Oh, crawling was pleasant, but rest is best."

He slept through the winter long and cold,
All tightly up in his blanket rolled,
And at last he awoke on a warm spring day
To find that winter had gone away.

He awoke to find he had golden wings,
And no longer need crawl over sticks and
        things.
"Oh, the earth is nice," said the glad butterfly,
"But the sky is best, when we learn to fly!"

UNKNOWN

The Butterbean Tent

All through the garden I went and went,
And I walked in under the butterbean tent.

The poles leaned up like a good tepee
And made a nice little house for me.

I had a hard brown clod for a seat,
And all outside was a cool green street.

A little green worm and a butterfly
And a cricket-like thing that could hop
    went by.

Hidden away there were flocks and flocks
Of bugs that could go like little clocks.

Such a good day it was when I spent
A long, long while in the butterbean tent.

ELIZABETH MADOX ROBERTS

79

The Grasshoppers

High
Up
Over the top
Of feathery grasses the
Grasshoppers hop.
They won't eat their suppers;
They will not obey
Their grasshopper mothers
And fathers, who say:
"Listen, my children,
This must be stopped—
Now is the time your last
Hop should be hopped;
So come eat your suppers
And go to your beds—"
But the little green grasshoppers
Shake their green heads.
"No
No—"
The naughty ones say
"All we have time to do
Now is to play.
If we want supper we'll
Nip at a fly
Or nibble a blueberry
As we go by;
If we feel sleepy we'll
Close our eyes tight
And snoozle away in a
Harebell all night.
But not
Now.
Now we must hop.
And nobody,
NOBODY,
Can make us stop."

DOROTHY ALDIS

Grasshopper Green

Grasshopper green is a comical chap;
   He lives on the best of fare.
Bright little trousers, jacket, and cap,
   These are his summer wear.
Out in the meadow he loves to go,
   Playing away in the sun;
It's hopperty, skipperty, high and low,
   Summer's the time for fun.

Grasshopper green has a quaint little house;
   It's under the hedge so gay.
Grandmother Spider, as still as a mouse,
   Watches him over the way.
Gladly he's calling the children, I know,
   Out in the beautiful sun;
It's hopperty, skipperty, high and low,
   Summer's the time for fun.

UNKNOWN

The Locust

Locust, locust, playing a flute,
Locust, locust, playing a flute!
   Away up above on the pine-tree bough,
     Closely clinging,
      Playing a flute,
      Playing a flute!

Trans. by FRANK CUSHING

The Cricket

And when the rain had gone away
And it was shining everywhere,
I ran out on the walk to play,
And found a little bug was there.

And he was running just as fast
As any little bug could run,
Until he stopped for breath at last,
All black and shiny in the sun.

And then he chirped a song to me
And gave his wings a little tug,
And *that's* the way he showed that he
Was very glad to be a bug!

MARJORIE BARROWS

Little Black Bug

Little black bug,
Little black bug,
Where have you been?
I've been under the rug,
Said little black bug.
Bug-ug-ug-ug.

Little green fly,
Little green fly,
Where have you been?
I've been way up high,
Said little green fly.
Bzzzzzzzzzzzzzzzzzz.

Little old mouse,
Little old mouse,
Where have you been?
I've been all through the house,
Said little old mouse.
Squeak-eak-eak-eak-eak.

MARGARET WISE BROWN

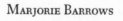

81

Fireflies

Little lamps of the dusk,
　　You fly low and gold
When the summer evening
　　Starts to unfold
So that all the insects,
　　Now, before you pass,
Will have light to see by
　　Undressing in the grass.

But when night has flowered,
　　Little lamps agleam,
You fly over treetops
　　Following a dream.
Men wonder from their windows
　　That a firefly goes so far—
They do not know your longing
　　To be a shooting star.

CAROLYN HALL

The Firefly Lights His Lamp

　　Although the night is damp,
The little firefly ventures out,
　　And slowly lights his lamp.

UNKNOWN (Japanese)

Under the Ground

　　What is under the grass,
　　Way down in the ground,
　　Where everything is cool and wet
　　With darkness all around?

　　Little pink worms live there;
　　Ants and brown bugs creep
　　Softly round the stones and rocks
　　Where roots are pushing deep.

　　Do they hear us walking
　　On the grass above their heads;
　　Hear us running over
　　While they snuggle in their beds?

RHODA W. BACMEISTER

Fireflies

I like to chase the fireflies,
　　Chase them to and fro;
I like to watch them dart about,
　　Their little lamps aglow.

In the evening's twilight dim
　　I follow them about;
I often think I have one caught,
　　And then his light goes out.

I cannot tell just where he is
　　Until he winks, you see,
Then far away I see his light—
　　He's played a joke on me.

GRACE WILSON COPLEN

The Worm

No, little worm, you need not slip
Into your hole, with such a skip;
Drawing the gravel as you glide
On to your smooth and slimy side.

I'm not a crow, poor worm, not I,
Peeping about your holes to spy,
And fly away with you in air,
To give my young ones each a share.

O no, I'm only looking about,
To see you wriggle in and out,
And drawing together your slimy rings,
Instead of feet, like other things:

So, little worm, don't slide and slip
Into your hole, with such a skip!

ANN TAYLOR

The Worm

When the earth is turned in spring
The worms are fat as anything.

And birds come flying all around
To eat the worms right off the ground.

They like worms just as much as I
Like bread and milk and apple pie.

And once, when I was very young,
I put a worm right on my tongue.

I didn't like the taste a bit,
And so I didn't swallow it.

But oh, it makes my Mother squirm
Because she *thinks* I ate that worm!

RALPH BERGENGREN

83

The Snare

I hear a sudden cry of pain!
There is a rabbit in a snare:
Now I hear the cry again,
But I cannot tell from where.

But I cannot tell from where
He is calling out for aid!
Crying on the frightened air,
Making everything afraid!

Making everything afraid!
Wrinkling up his little face!
As he cries again for aid;
—And I cannot find the place!

And I cannot find the place
Where his paw is in the snare!
Little One! Oh, Little One!
I am searching everywhere!

JAMES STEPHENS

The Rabbit

The rabbit has a habit
  Of sitting on his heels
With his little paws in front of him;
  I wonder how it feels.

The grasses where he passes
  He nibbles if they suit,
And he nips the tips of daisies,
  Or he chews a tender root.

He rollicks and he frolics
  In a very cunning way;
When the moon shines white upon him;
  But he loves to sleep by day.

His hole is where the mole is:
  Down beneath the maple tree;
Twisting in and out and round about,
  As safe as it can be.

GEORGIA ROBERTS DURSTON

Little Things

Little things, that run, and quail,
And die, in silence and despair!

Little things, that fight, and fail,
And fall, on sea, and earth, and air!

All trapped and frightened little things,
The mouse, the coney, hear our prayer!

As we forgive those done to us,
—The lamb, the linnet, and the hare—

Forgive us all our trespasses,
Little creatures, everywhere!

JAMES STEPHENS

The Rabbits' Song Outside the Tavern

We, who play under the pines,
We, who dance in the snow
That shines blue in the light of the moon,
Sometimes halt as we go—
Stand with our ears erect,
Our noses testing the air,
To gaze at the golden world
Behind the windows there.

Suns they have in a cave,
Stars, each on a tall white stem,
And the thought of a fox or an owl
Seems never to trouble them.
They laugh and eat and are warm,
Their food is ready at hand,
While hungry out in the cold
We little rabbits stand.

But they never dance as we dance!
They haven't the speed nor the grace.
We scorn both the dog and the cat
Who lie by their fireplace.
We scorn them licking their paws
Their eyes on an upraised spoon—
We who dance hungry and wild
Under a winter's moon.

ELIZABETH COATSWORTH

A Rabbit

A rabbit works its ears, and tries
To watch you with its rabbit eyes;
Its saucy tail it flounces,
And when it hits the ground, it bounces.

MARY CAROLYN DAVIES

Little Brown Bear

Woof! Woof! Woof!
Brown bear—Yum!
Here is honey
Come—eat some!

I know you like it
Because it's good—
Little brown bear,
Living in the wood.

ALICE WILKINS

Colts

Colts behind their mothers
Trot across the plain,
Rustling, zoro-zoro, like a lady's train.

JAPANESE HOKKU

The Wolf

When the pale moon hides and the wild wind
        wails,
And over the tree-tops the nighthawk sails,
The gray wolf sits on the world's far rim,
And howls: and it seems to comfort him.

The wolf is a lonely soul, you see,
No beast in the wood, nor bird in the tree,
But shuns his path; in the windy gloom
They give him plenty, and plenty of room.

So he sits with his long, lean face to the sky
Watching the ragged clouds go by.
There in the night, alone, apart,
Singing the song of his lone, wild heart.

Far away, on the world's dark rim
He howls, and it seems to comfort him.

GEORGIA ROBERTS DURSTON

A Little Squirrel

I saw a little squirrel,
Sitting in a tree;
He was eating a nut
And wouldn't look at me.

               Child in Winnetka Nursery

Kindness to Animals

Little children, never give
Pain to things that feel and live;
Let the gentle robin come
For the crumbs you save at home,—
As his meat you throw along
He'll repay you with a song;
Never hurt the timid hare
Peeping from her green grass lair,
Let her come and sport and play
On the lawn at close of day;
The little lark goes soaring high
To the bright windows of the sky,
Singing as if 'twere always spring,
And fluttering on an untired wing,—
Oh! let him sing his happy song,
Nor do these gentle creatures wrong.

                        Unknown

Overtones

I heard a bird at break of day
   Sing from the autumn trees
A song so mystical and calm,
   So full of certainties,
No man, I think, could listen long
   Except upon his knees.
Yet this was but a simple bird,
   Alone, among dead trees.

            William Alexander Percy

People Buy A Lot of Things

People buy a lot of things—
Carts and balls and nails and rings,
But I would buy a bird that sings.

I would buy a bird that sings and let it sing
   for me,
And let it sing of flying things and mating in
   a tree,
And then I'd open wide the cage, and set the
   singer free.

                  Annette Wynne

Humming-Bird

Why do you stand on the air
And no sun shining?
How can you hold yourself so still
On raindrops sliding?
They change and fall, they are not steady,
But you do not know they are gone.
Is there a silver wire
I cannot see?
Is the wind your perch?
Raindrops slide down your little shoulders . . .
They do not wet you.
I think you are not real
In your green feathers!
You are not a humming-bird at all
Standing on air above the garden!
I dreamed you the way I dream fairies,
Or the flower I lost yesterday!

HILDA CONKLING

Woodpecker With Long Ears

The woodpecker there in that tree
Discombobulates me!
He keeps knocking and knocking and
knocking till I
Get so angry! For why
Can't he see
There's no door in that tree?
He knocks all around
From the top to the ground
On the trunk. Then flies out on a limb.
It's so foolish of him!
If I'd knocked on one tree
As often as he,
I'd make up my mind
There was no door to find.
If I knocked any more
It would be
On some other tree
That might have a door
I could see.

TOM ROBINSON

The Secret

We have a secret, just we three,
The robin, and I, and the sweet cherry-tree;
The bird told the tree, and the tree told me,
And nobody knows it but just us three.

But of course the robin knows it best,
Because he built the—I shan't tell the rest;
And laid the four little—something in it—
I'm afraid I shall tell it every minute.

But if the tree and the robin don't peep,
I'll try my best the secret to keep;
Though I know when the little birds fly about
Then the whole secret will be out.

UNKNOWN

The Robin

When father takes his spade to dig
Then Robin comes along;
He sits upon a little twig
And sings a little song.

Or, if the trees are rather far
He does not stay alone,
But comes up close to where we are
And bobs upon a stone.

LAWRENCE ALMA-TADEMA

89

The Blackbird

In the far corner
close by the swings,
every morning
a blackbird sings.

His bill's so yellow,
his coat's so black,
that he makes a fellow
whistle back.

Ann, my daughter,
thinks that he
sings for us two
especially.

HUMBERT WOLFE

The Birds' Nests

The skylark's nest among the grass
    And waving corn is found;
The robin's on a shady bank,
    With oak leaves strewn around.

The wren builds in an ivied thorn,
    Or old and ruined wall;
The mossy nest, so covered in,
    You scarce can see at all.

The martins build their nests of clay,
    In rows beneath the eaves;
While silvery lichens, moss, and hair,
    The chaffinch interweaves.

The cuckoo makes no nest at all,
    But through the wood she strays
Until she finds one snug and warm,
    And there her eggs she lays.

The sparrow has a nest of hay,
    With feathers warmly lined;
The ringdove's careless nest of sticks
    On lofty trees we find.

Rooks build together in a wood,
    And often disagree;
The owl will build inside a barn
    Or in a hollow tree.

The blackbird's nest of grass and mud
    In brush and bank is found;
The lapwing's darkly spotted eggs
    Are laid upon the ground.

The magpie's nest is girt with thorns
    In leafless tree or hedge;
The wild duck and the water hen
Build by the water's edge.

Birds build their nests from year to year,
    According to their kind—
Some very neat and beautiful,
    Some easily designed.

The habits of each little bird,
    And all its patient skill,
Are surely taught by God himself
    And ordered by His will.

ANONYMOUS

90

The Sandpiper

Across the narrow beach we flit,
 One little sandpiper and I,
And fast I gather, bit by bit,
 The scattered driftwood bleached and dry.
The wild waves reach their hands for it,
 The wild wind raves, the tide runs high,
As up and down the beach we flit,—
 One little sandpiper and I.

Above our heads the sullen clouds
 Scud black and swift across the sky;
Like silent ghosts in misty shrouds
 Stand out the white lighthouses high.
Almost as far as eye can reach
 I see the close-reefed vessels fly,
As fast we flit along the beach,—
 One little sandpiper and I.

I watch him as he skims along,
 Uttering his sweet and mournful cry.
He starts not at my fitful song,
 Nor flash of fluttering drapery.
He has no thought of any wrong;
 He scans me with a fearless eye:
Staunch friends are we, well tried and strong,
 The little sandpiper and I.

Comrade, where wilt thou be tonight,
 When the loosed storm breaks furiously?
My driftwood fire will burn so brightly!
 To what warm shelter canst thou fly?
I do not fear for thee, though wroth
 The tempest rushes through the sky:
For are we not God's children both,
 Thou, little sandpiper, and I?

CELIA THAXTER

The Snow-Bird

When all the ground with snow is white,
  The merry snow-bird comes,
And hops about with great delight
  To find the scattered crumbs.

How glad he seems to get to eat
  A piece of cake or bread!
He wears no shoes upon his feet,
  Nor hat upon his head.

But happiest is he, I know,
  Because no cage with bars
Keeps him from walking on the snow
  And printing it with stars.

FRANK DEMPSTER SHERMAN

The Sea Gull

I watched the pretty, white sea gull
Come riding into town;
The waves came up when he came up,
Went down when he went down.

LEROY F. JACKSON

WHITHER DO YOU WANDER

Jump or Jiggle

Frogs jump
Caterpillars hump

Worms wiggle
Bugs jiggle

Rabbits hop
Horses clop

Snakes slide
Seagulls glide

Mice creep
Deer leap

Puppies bounce
Kittens pounce

Lions stalk—
But—
I walk!

EVELYN BEYER

Traveling Light

Mister Robin and his wife have started south
    once more
They didn't shut a window, and they didn't
    lock a door!
They didn't take a traveling-bag or lunch or
    anything!
Just took themselves! And said, "Cheerup!
  We'll be back next spring!"

MINNIE LEONA UPTON

Susan Blue

Oh, Susan Blue,
  How do you do?
Please may I walk with you?
  Where shall we go?
  Oh, I know—
Down in the meadow where the cowslips grow!

KATE GREENAWAY

Summer Rapture

I shall climb a green hill,
With summer winds above it;
And shall loose my chestnut hair;
And I shall love it!

Oh, I shall climb a green hill,
With clover blossoms scented;
And weave a garland frail and fair;
And be contented!

Oh, I shall climb a green hill,
And when I reach the summit,
I'll find a little song there;
And I shall hum it!

WINIFRED GRAY STEWART

94

How Creatures Move

The lion walks on padded paws
The squirrel leaps from limb to limb
While flies can crawl straight up a wall
And seals can dive and swim.
The worm he wiggles all around
The monkey swings by his tail
And birds may hop upon the ground
Or spread their wings and sail.
But boys and girls
Have much more fun;
They leap and dance
And walk and run.

UNKNOWN

There Are So Many Ways of Going Places

Big yellow trolley lumbers along,
Long black subway sings an under song,
Airplanes swoop and flash in the sky,
Noisy old elevated goes rocketing by.
Boats across the water—back and forth they go,
Big boats and little boats, fast boats and slow.
Trains puff and thunder; their engines have
    a headlight;
They have a special kind of car where you can
    sleep all night.
Tall fat busses on the Avenue,
They will stop for anyone—even—just—you.
All kinds of autos rush down the street.
And then there are always—your own two feet.

LESLIE THOMPSON

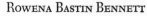

The Station

The station is a busy place,
With miles and miles of trains,
That run all day and every night
And even when it rains.

There're lots and lots of people there,
With bags and boxes too,
And lots of men to carry them,
All dressed alike in blue.

And when you hear the whistle blow,
Along there comes a train,
And everyone calls out goodbye,
And kisses me again.

KITTY PARSONS

A Modern Dragon

A train is a dragon that roars through the dark.
He wriggles his tail as he sends up a spark.
He pierces the night with his one yellow eye,
And all the earth trembles when he rushes by.

ROWENA BASTIN BENNETT

I Meant To do My Work Today

I meant to do my work today—
But a brown bird sang in the apple tree,
And a butterfly flitted across the field,
And all the leaves were calling me.

And the wind went sighing over the land
Tossing the grasses to and fro,
And a rainbow held out its shining hand—
So what could I do but laugh and go?

RICHARD LE GALLIENNE

Which?

Whenever I'm walking in the wood
I'm never certain whether I should
Shuffle along where the dead leaves fall
Or walk as if I'm not there at all.

It's nice to rustle as hard as you can,
But I can't decide if it's nicer than
Creeping along, while the woodbirds call,
Pretending you are not there at all!

JOYCE L. BRISLEY

Roads

A road might lead to anywhere—
    To harbor towns and quays,
Or to a witch's painted house
    Hidden by bristly trees.
It might lead past the tailor's door,
    Where he sews with needle and thread,
Or by Miss Pim the milliner's,
    With her hats for every head.
It might be a road to a great, dark cave
    With treasure and gold piled high,
Or a road with a mountain tied to its end,
    Blue-humped against the sky.
Oh, a road might lead you to anywhere—
    To Mexico or Maine;
But then, it might just fool you, and
    Lead you back home again!

RACHEL FIELD

When I Grow Up

When I grow up I mean to go
Where all the biggest rivers flow,
And take a ship and sail around
The Seven Seas until I've found
Robinson Crusoe's famous isle,
And there I'll land and stay a while,
And see how it would feel to be
Lord on an island in the sea.

When I grow up I mean to rove
Through orange and palmetto grove,
To drive a sledge across the snow
Where great explorers go,
To hunt for treasures hid of old
By buccaneers and pirates bold,
And see if somewhere there may be
A mountain no one's climbed but me.

When I grow up I mean to do
The things I've always wanted to;
I don't see why grown people stay
At home when they could be away.

RUPERT SARGENT HOLLAND

A Summer Walk

A little girl went for a walk
  One pleasant summer day;
She walked so far and very fast
  She truly ran away.

At last she came to a small pond
  A pond both small and round;
And looking wonderingly about
  She heard a curious sound.

  "You'd better-go-home—
  You'd better-go-home!"
The words seemed plainly said.
No man or woman could she see—
  She surely felt afraid.

  "You'd better-go-home—
  You'd better-go-home!"
The words came o'er and o'er.
  The little girl then turned and ran
As she never ran before.

  "You'd better-go-home—
  You'd better-go-home!"
Kept ringing from the bog;
  "You'd better-go-home—
  You'd better-go-home!"
The words came from a frog.

ELIZABETH WINTON

Millions of Strawberries

Marcia and I went over the curve,
Eating our way down
Jewels of strawberries we didn't deserve,
Eating our way down,
Till our hands were sticky, and our lips
    painted.
And over us the hot day fainted,
And we saw snakes,
And got scratched,
And a lust overcame us for the red unmatched
Small buds of berries,
Till we lay down—
Eating our way down—
And rolled in the berries like two little dogs,
Rolled
In the late gold.
And gnats hummed,
And it was cold,
And home we went, home without a berry,
Painted red and brown,
Eating our way down.

GENEVIEVE TAGGARD

The Wagon in the Barn

There are mushrooms in the paddock,
   And walnuts on the trees,
And a hive in the corner
   To keep the honey-bees;
There's a hay-rick in the rick-yard,
   And another one of wheat,
And there are cooking apples,
   And other ones to eat.

There are berries on the bushes,
   The yellow ones and red,
There are starlings in the willows,
   And swallows in the shed;
There's a scarecrow in the garden,
   With a patch upon his starn,
But the thing that I like best is
   The wagon in the barn.

For in the rainy weather,
   We all climb up inside,
And we have a team of horses
   To take us for a ride;
And although they think we're playing
   In the barn because it rains,
We go riding in the wagon
   For miles along the lanes.

JOHN DRINKWATER

The Naughty Boy

There was a naughty boy,
   And a naughty boy was he,
He ran away to Scotland
   The people for to see—
     Then he found
     That the ground
     Was as hard,
     That a yard
     Was as long,
     That a song
     Was as merry,
     That a cherry
     Was as red,
     That lead
     Was as weighty,
     That fourscore
     Was eighty,
     That a door
     Was as wooden
     As in England—
So he stood in his shoes
   And he wondered,
   He wondered.
He stood in his shoes
   And he wondered.

JOHN KEATS

The Road To China

I learned today the world is round
   Like my big rubber ball,
With China on the other side,
   Down there below us all.

And so I went and dug a hole,—
   I started in at eight,—
And dug and dug and dug and dug,
   Beside the garden gate.

And oh, I thought, what fun 'twill be
   To get a ladder tall,
And climb right down to China through
   The hole behind the wall!

What fun to walk through little streets
   All lit with lanterns queer!
Each man will have a pigtail, and
   How strange the talk I'll hear!

To think the road to China lies
   Just by our garden wall!
Then Daddy came and said, "Ho! Ho!
   That's not the way at all!

"To get to China, you must sail
   For days across the sea!"
Why there's no short cut through the earth
   Seems very queer to me!

And still I sit beside my hole
   And dream and dream away,
Of that strange, far-off country where
   They've night time in our day!

OLIVE BEAUPRE MILLER

Moving

I like to move. There's such a feeling
Of hurrying
   and scurrying,
And such a feeling
Of men with trunks and packing cases,
Of kitchen clocks and mother's laces,
Dusters, dishes, books, and vases,
Toys and pans and candles.

I always find things I'd forgotten:
An old brown Teddy stuffed with cotton,
Some croquet mallets without handles,
A marble and my worn-out sandals,
A half an engine and a hat . . .
And I like that.

I like to watch the big vans backing,
And the lumbering
   and the cumbering,
And the hammering and the tacking.
I even like the packing.

And that will prove
I like to move!

EUNICE TIETJENS

99

In the evening from my window
  Just before I go to bed
I can watch the trains a-gliding
  Beneath the stars that shine o'erhead.
Far away, the engine seems a beetle black
Drawing lines of flowing fireflies on a track.

How I wonder where they are going,
  What they will see before the day,
Mighty mountains, lonely forests,
  Sleeping cities far away.
Arching bridges, long, long trestles
  They'll pass o'er
Plunging into darksome tunnels with a roar.

UNKNOWN

The Airplane

The airplane taxies down the field
And heads into the breeze,
It lifts its wheels above the ground,
It skims above the trees,
It rises high and higher
Away up toward the sun,
It's just a speck against the sky
  —And now it's gone!

MARY McB. GREEN

The Zeppelin

The Zeppelin, the Zeppelin!
  He has a fish's tail
And a fish's nose, so I suppose
  He does not need a sail.

The Zeppelin, the Zeppelin!
  He is a flying fish.
The foamy waves break over him,
  The little breezes swish
Against him like the sea waves.
Oh, how he loves to swim
Across the sky, and some day I
  Shall take a ride on him.

ROWENA BASTIN BENNETT

The Fog Horn

Foggy, foggy, over the water,
Foggy, foggy, over the bay,
Foggy, so foggy the boats are like shadows
And how can they find their way?

Far away and over the water
Hear the voice of the fog horn say
"Whoo-oo-oo, I'm guiding you,
Boats that are out on the bay."

Foggy, foggy over the water,
Foggy, foggy over the bay,
And through the fog the boats go slowly
While the fog horn tells them the way.

EDITH H. NEWLIN

Riding in a Motor Boat

A putta putta putt—
The motor boat
Splashes
A spray behind it.

A putta putta putt—
I go for a ride
And watch
The beach slide by.

I see a man upside down on his head,
And a boy turning somersaults,
And umbrellas
That stand
Like high mushrooms
In the sand.

A putta putt putt—
I reach my hand
Over the side of the boat
Into the slipping water.

It feels
Tingly
And cold.

DOROTHY W. BARUCH

Waters

Sprinkling
Wrinkling
Softly tinkling
Twinkling
Tiny brook,
Running
Funning
Hiding, sunning
Cunning baby brook,
Joins a grownup brook.
Dashing
Splashing
Sunlight flashing
Stony grownup brook

Joins the river
Broad smooth river
Deep as deep can be.
Slower, slower, slower flowing,
Wider—wider—wider—growing,
Till it empties all its waters out into the great
huge sea.
Rolling,—rolling,—tossing,—rolling,
Splashing waves forever rolling in the great
wide sea.

EDITH H. NEWLIN

The Edge of the World

From the top of the bluff, where the wind
blows free,
Clear out to the edge of the world I see,
And I look and look, till my eyes grow dim,
But I can't see what lies over the rim!

I see the steamers go in towards town;
I watch the schooners sail slowly down—
Down out of sight, and far away—
Oh! I shall sail over the rim, some day.

Over the rim and far beyond,
To Hong Kong and Bagdad and Trebizond,
And Ceylon's Isle, where the breezes blow,
And the Happy Harbor, where good ships go.

And it may be bad, or it may be fair,
And I may come back, or I may stay there,
But one thing is sure—be it gay or grim,
Some day—some day—I must cross that rim!

MARY FANNY YOUNGS

Shore

Play on the seashore
And gather up shells,
Kneel in the damp sands
Digging wells.

Run on the rocks
Where the seaweed slips,
Watch the waves
And the beautiful ships.

MARY BRITTON MILLER

At the Sea-Side

When I was down beside the sea
A wooden spade they gave to me
To dig the sandy shore.

My holes were empty like a cup.
In every hole the sea came up,
Till it could come no more.

ROBERT LOUIS STEVENS

Adventure

I went slowly through the wood of shadows,
Thinking always I should meet some one:
There was no one.

I found a hollow
Sweet to rest in all night long:
I did not stay.

I came out beyond the trees
To the moaning sea.
Over the sea swam a cloud the outline of a ship:
What if that ship held my adventure
Under its sails?

Come quickly to me, come quickly,
I am waiting;
I am here on the sand.
Sail close!
I want to go over the waves . . .
The sand holds me back.
Oh adventure, if you belong to me,
Don't blow away down the sky!

HILDA CONKLING

On the Bridge

If I could see a little fish—
That is what I just now wish!
I want to see his great round eyes
Always open in surprise.

I wish a water rat would glide
Slowly to the other side;
Or a dancing spider sit
On the yellow flags a bit.

I think I'll get some stones to throw,
And watch the pretty circles show.
Or shall we sail a flower boat,
And watch it slowly—slowly float?

That's nice—because you never know
How far away it means to go;
And when tomorrow comes, you see,
It may be in the great wide sea.

KATE GREENAWAY

Paper Boats

Day by day I float my paper boats one by one down the running stream.

In big black letters I write my name on them and the name of the village where I live.

I hope that some one in some strange land will find them and know who I am.
I load my little boats with *shiuli* flowers from our garden, and hope that these blooms of dawn will be carried safely to land in the night.

I launch my paper boats and look up into the sky and see the little clouds setting their white bulging sails.

I know not what playmate of mine in the sky sends them down the air to race with my boats.

When night comes I bury my face in my arms and dream that my paper boats float on and on under the midnight stars.

The fairies of sleep are sailing in them, and the lading is their baskets full of dreams.

RABINDRANATH TAGORE

FAIRIES AND WISHES

Children, Children, Don't Forget

Children, children, don't forget
There are elves and fairies yet;
Where the knotty hawthorn grows
Look for prints of fairy toes.
Where the grassy rings are green
Moonlight dances shall be seen.
Watch and wait: O lucky you,
If you find a fairy shoe:
For a ransom he will pay,
Hobbling barefoot all the day,
Lay it on his mushroom seat,
Wish your wish and go your way
If your wish should be discreet
Never fear but he will pay.

DORA OWEN

Fairy Wings

Through the windmills
Fairies weave
Stuff for wings
From the breath
Of the winds
On the hills.

From the South
Comes the blue;
From the West
Saffron hue;
From the East
Comes the rose,
And the North
Brings the silver
From the snows.

Colours blended,
Dainty, fair;
Silken fabric
Light as air.

They fashion as wings,
And spread them to catch
The sunshine at noon;
Dip into dew,
And hang them to dry,
On a clear frosty night,
From the beams of the moon.

WINIFRED HOWARD

The Fairy Frock

It's primrose petals for a gown,
For sempstress spiders three,
It's gossamer and thistledown
To make my frock for me.
Then hie thee straight to cobbler toad
Beneath the hornbeam tree
Beyond the turning of the road
To shape my shoes for me.
Then put a dewdrop in my hair,
Fetch me my cobweb shawl,
And call my cricket coach and pair
To drive me to the ball!

KATHARINE MORSE

The Popcorn Party

In little white dresses and little white pants
Girl fairies, boy fairies join in the dance,
One-stepping, waltzing, faster and higher,
On a floor made of holes, over red and gold fire!

E.R.B.

Godmother

There was an old lady
Who had three faces,
One for everyday,
And one for wearing places—
To meetings and parties,
Dull places like that—
A face that looked well
With a grown-up hat.
But she carried in her pocket
The face of an elf,
And she'd clap it on quick
When she felt like herself.
Sitting in the parlor
Of somebody's house,
She'd reach in her pocket
Sly as a mouse . . .
And there in the corner,
Sipping her tea,
Was a laughing elf-woman
Nobody could see!

PHYLLIS B. MORDEN

The Angel in the Apple Tree

Early in the morning, before the day began,
   Out along the hillside, glittering and cold
And out into the orchard that was all dim gold,
Barefoot, and by myself, breathlessly I ran.

There I saw an angel resting in an apple tree,
   A lovely, silver Person up among the leaves—
     From deep in the folds of one of her blue
      sleeves,
She took a yellow apple, and she dropped it
     down to me.

I clasped my hands around it, I lifted up
     my eyes
     To smile at her and thank her, but already
      she was gone.
     I stood among the grasses very still and all
      alone—
While the green leaves rustled and the sun
     began to rise.

WINIFRED WELLES

Vision

I've seen her, I've seen her
Beneath an apple tree;
The minute that I saw her there
With stars and dewdrops in her hair,
I knew it must be she.
She's sitting on a dragon-fly
All shining green and gold,
A little way above the ground;
The dragon-fly goes circling round—
She isn't taking hold.

I've seen her, I've seen her—
I never, never knew
That anything could be so sweet;
She has the tiniest hands and feet,
Her wings are very blue.
She holds her little head like this,
Because she is a queen;
(I can't describe it all in words)
She's throwing kisses to the birds
And laughing in between.

I've seen her, I've seen her—
I simply ran and ran;
Put down your sewing quickly, please,
Let's hurry to the orchard trees
As softly as we can.
I had to go and leave her there,
I felt I couldn't stay,—
I wanted you to see her, too—
But, oh, whatever shall we do
If she has flown away?

ROSE FYLEMAN

Crab-Apple

I dreamed the Fairies wanted me
   To spend my birth-night with them all;
And I said, "Oh, but you're so wee
   And I am so tremendous tall,
What could we do?"
   "Crab-apple stem!"
Said they, and I was just like them.

And then, when we were all the same,
   The party and the fun began;
They said they'd teach me a new game
   Of "Dew-ponds." "I don't think I can
Play that," I said.
   "Crab-apple blue!"
Said they, and I could play it too.

And then when we had played and played,
   The Fairies said that we would dance;
And I said, "Oh, but I'm afraid
   That I've no shoes." I gave a glance
At my bare toes.
   "Crab-apple sweet!"
Said they, and shoes were on my feet.

And then we danced away, away,
   Until my birth-night all was done;
And I said, "I'll go home to-day;
   And thank you for my lovely fun,
I'll come again."
   "Crab-apple red!"
Said they, and I woke up in bed.

ETHEL TALBOT

The Elf and the Dormouse

Under a toadstool crept a wee Elf,
Out of the rain to shelter himself.

Under the toadstool, sound asleep,
Sat a big Dormouse all in a heap.

Trembled the wee Elf, frightened, and yet
Fearing to fly away lest he get wet.

To the next shelter—maybe a mile!
Sudden the wee Elf smiled a wee smile,

Tugged till the toadstool toppled in two.
Holding it over him, gaily he flew.

Soon he was safe home, dry as could be.
Soon woke the Dormouse—"Good gracious me!

"Where is my toadstool?" loud he lamented.
—And that's how umbrellas first were invented.

OLIVER HERFORD

The Little Elf

I met a little Elf-man, once,
    Down where the lilies blow.
I asked him why he was so small,
    And why he didn't grow.

He slightly frowned, and with his eye
    He looked me through and through.
"I'm quite as big for me," said he,
    "As you are big for you."

JOHN KENDRICK BANGS

The Piper

Piping down the valleys wild,
    Piping songs of pleasant glee,
On a cloud I saw a child,
    And he laughing said to me:

"Pipe a song about a lamb!"
    So I piped with merry cheer.
"Piper, pipe that song again;"
    So I piped: he wept to hear.

"Drop thy pipe, thy happy pipe;
    Sing thy songs of happy cheer!"
So I sang the same again,
    While he wept with joy to hear.

"Piper, sit thee down and write
    In a book that all may read."
So he vanished from my sight;
    And I plucked a hollow reed,

And I made a rural pen,
    And I stained the water clear,
And I wrote my happy songs
    Every child may joy to hear.

WILLIAM BLAKE

And maybe his heart went dreaming,
  Or maybe his thoughts went wide,
But he took his battered old fiddle
  And he took the bow from his side.

And he said, "I will play them such music
  As never a fairy heard."
He said, "I will play them the music
  I stole from the throat of a bird."

And the sound of his lilt went straying
  By valley and stream and sedge
Till the little white stars went dancing
  Along the mountain's edge.

And things came out of the bushes
  And out of the grassy mound
And joined their hands in a circle
  And danced to the fiddle's sound.

And quicker and sweeter and stranger
  The notes came hurrying out
And joined with a shriek and a whistle
  In the dance of the Goblin Rout.

And all night long on the green lands
  They danced in a 'wildered ring.
And every note of the fiddle
  Was the shriek of a godless thing.

And when the winter morning
  Came whitely up the glen,
The Fiddler's soul fled whistling
  In the rout of the Fairy Men.

Seumas O'Sullivan

The Ballad of the Fiddler

He had played by the cottage fire
  Till the dancing all was done,
But his heart kept up the music
  When the last folk had gone.

So he came through the half-door softly
  And wandered up the hill,
In the glow of his heart's desire
  That was on the music still.

And he passed the blackthorn thicket,
  And he heard the branches groan,
As they bowed beneath the burden
  Of the white fruit of the moon.

And he came to the fairy circle
  Where none but the wise may sit:
And blindness was on him surely
  For he sat in the midst of it.

Invitation

Let's play we are a tune
And make a kind of song
About the sun and moon
Before the stars were born.
You be the breath, I'll be the horn,
It will not take us long.

Ridgely Torrence

The Fairies

Up the airy mountain,
　Down the rushy glen,
We daren't go a-hunting
　For fear of little men;

Wee folk, good folk,
　Trooping all together;
Green jacket, red cap,
　And white owl's feather!

Down along the rocky shore
　Some make their home,
They live on crispy pancakes
　Of yellow tide-foam;

Some in the reeds
　Of the black mountain lake,
With frogs for their watch-dogs,
　All night awake.

High on the hill-top
　The old King sits;
He is now so old and gray
　He's nigh lost his wits.

With a bridge of white mist
　Columbkill he crosses,
On his stately journeys
　From Slieveleague to Rosses;

Or going up with music
　On cold starry nights
To sup with the Queen
　Of the gay Northern Lights.

They stole little Bridget
　For seven years long;
When she came down again
　Her friends were all gone.
They took her lightly back,

　Between the night and morrow,
They thought that she was fast asleep,
　But she was dead with sorrow.

They have kept her ever since
　Deep within the lake,
On a bed of flag-leaves,
　Watching till she wake.

By the craggy hill-side,
　Through the mosses bare,
They have planted thorn-trees
　For pleasure here and there.

If any man so daring
　As dig them up in spite,
He shall find their sharpest thorns
　In his bed at night.

Up the airy mountain,
　Down the rushy glen,
We daren't go a-hunting
　For fear of little men;

Wee folk, good folk,
　Trooping all together;
Green jacket, red cap,
　And white owl's feather.

WILLIAM ALLINGHAM

Morning and evening
Maids hear the goblins cry:
"Come buy our orchard fruits,
Come buy, come buy:
Apples and quinces,
Lemons and oranges,
Plump unpecked cherries,
Melons and raspberries,
Bloom-down-cheeked peaches,
Swart-headed mulberries,
Wild free-born cranberries,
Crab-apples, dewberries,
Pine-apples, blackberries,
Apricots, strawberries;—
All ripe together
In summer weather,—
Morns that pass by,
Fair eves that fly;
Come buy, come buy:
Our grapes fresh from the vine,
Pomegranates full and fine,
Dates and sharp bullaces,
Rare pears and greengages,
Damsons and bilberries,
Taste them and try:
Currants and gooseberries,
Bright-fire-like barberries,
Figs to fill your mouth,
Citrons from the South,
Sweet to tongue and sound to eye;
Come buy, come buy."

CHRISTINA ROSSETTI

Water Lily

I'd like to be a water-lily sleeping on the river,
Where solemn rushes whisper, and funny
    ripples quiver,
All day I'd watch the blue sky—all night I'd
    watch the black,
Floating in the soft waves, dreaming on my
    back.

And when I'd tire of dreaming, I'd call a
    passing fish,
"I want to find the sea!" I'd shout. "Come! you
    can grant my wish!"
He'd bite me from my moorings, and softly I
    would slip
To the center of the river, like an ocean-going
    ship.

The waves would lash upon me. The wind
    would blow me fast,
And, oh, what shores and wonders would greet
    me as I passed!
Yes, if I were a water-lily, I'd sail to sea
    in state—
A green frog for my captain, and a dragon fly
    for mate!

JOHN FARRAR

The Merman

I

Who would be
A merman bold,
Sitting alone,
Singing alone
Under the sea,
With a crown of gold,
On a throne?

II

I would be a merman bold;
I would sit and sing the whole of the day;
I would fill the sea-halls with a voice of power
But at night I would roam abroad and play
With the mermaids in and out of the rocks,
Dressing their hair with the white sea-flower;
And holding them back by their flowing locks
I would kiss them often under the sea,
And kiss them again, till they kissed me
    Laughingly, laughingly;
And then we would wander away, away,
To the pale sea-groves straight and high
    Chasing each other merrily.

ALFRED TENNYSON

The Mermaid

I

Who would be
A mermaid fair,
Singing alone,
Combing her hair
Under the sea,
In a golden curl
With a comb of pearl,
On a throne?

II

I would be a mermaid fair;
I would sing to myself the whole of the day;
With a comb of pearl I would comb my hair;
And still as I combed I would sing and say,
"Who is it loves me? who loves not me?"
I would comb my hair till my ringlets would
    fall,
    Low adown, low adown,
And I should look like a fountain of gold
    Springing alone
    With a shrill inner sound
    Over the throne
    In the midst of the hall.

ALFRED TENNYSON

114

Shell Castles

A sea shell is a castle
Where a million echoes roam,
   A wee castle,
   Sea castle,
Tossed up by the foam;
   A wee creature's
   Sea creature's
Long deserted home.

If I were very tiny,
   I should walk those winding halls
And listen to the voices
   In the pink and pearly walls;
And each mysterious echo
   Would tell me salty tales
Of the phosphorescent fishes
And the white-winged ship that sails
   On the sea's brim
   Round the earth's rim
To the lilting of the gales;
   Of the sea horse
   That's a wee horse
And frolics in the sea
   'Neath the coral
   White and sorrel
That is the mermaids' tree;
   And grazes on the seaweed
   And the sea anemone;
But my ears cannot distinguish
   The words it sings to me,
     The sea shell
     The wee shell,
   I hold so reverently,
And I only hear a whisper
   Like the ghost voice of the sea.

ROWENA BASTIN BENNETT

The Sea Princess

In a garden of shining sea-weed,
   Set round with twisted shells,
Under the deeps of the ocean,
   The little sea princess dwells.

Sometimes she sees the shadow
   Of a great whale passing by,
Or a white-winged vessel sailing
   Between the sea and sky.

Without the palace, her sea-horse
   Feeds in his crystal stall,
And fishes, with scales that glisten,
   Come leaping forth at her call.

And when the day has faded
   From over the lonesome deep,
In a shell as smooth as satin
   The princess is rocked to sleep.

KATHARINE PYLE

Minnie and Winnie

Minnie and Winnie slept in a shell.
Sleep, little ladies! And they slept very well.

Pink was the shell within, silver without;
Sounds of the great sea wandered about.

Sleep, little ladies! Wake not soon!
Echo on echo dies to the moon.

Two bright stars peeped into the shell.
"What are they dreaming of? Who can tell?"

Started a green linnet out of the croft;
Wake, little ladies! The sun is aloft.

ALFRED TENNYSON

Overheard on a Saltmarsh

Nymph, nymph, what are your beads?
Green glass, goblin. Why do you stare at them?
Give them me.
      No.

Give them me. Give them me.

      No.

I will howl all night in the reeds,
Lie in the mud and howl for them.
Goblin, why do you love them so?
They are better than stars or water,
Better than voices of winds that sing,
Better than any man's fair daughter,
Your green glass beads on a silver ring.
Hush, I stole them out of the moon.
Give me your beads, I desire them.

      No.

I will howl in a deep lagoon
For your green glass beads, I love them so.
Give them me. Give them.

      No.

                    HAROLD MONRO

White Horses

Little white horses are out on the sea,
    Bridled with rainbows and speckled with
        foam,
Laden with presents for you and for me;
    Mermaids and fairies are riding them home!
        Gold from the sun;
        Diamonds rare
        Made from dew
        And frosty air;
        Veils of mist,
        Soft and white,
        Rose and silver,
        Shimmering, bright;
        Sweetest perfumes,
        Coloured shells,
        Lilting music,
        Fairy bells:
Fairies and mermaids are bringing them home
On little white horses all speckled with
        foam.

                    WINIFRED HOWARD

Sea Shell

Sea Shell, Sea Shell,
    Sing me a song, O please!
A song of ships, and sailor men,
    And parrots, and tropical trees,

Of islands lost in the Spanish Main
Which no man ever may find again,
Of Fishes and corals under the waves,
And sea-horses stabled in great green caves.

Sea Shell, Sea Shell,
Sing of the things you know so well.

                    AMY LOWELL

Treasures

Down on the beach when the tide is out
Beautiful things lie all about—
Rubies and diamonds and shells and pearls,
Starfish, oysters, and mermaids' curls;
Slabs of black marble cut in the sand,
Veined and smoothed and polished by hand;
And whipped-up foam that I think must be
What mermen use for cream in tea.

These and a million treasures I know
Strew the beach when the tide is low—
But very few people seem to care
For such gems scattered everywhere.
Lots of these jewels I hide away
In an old box I found one day.
And if a beggar asks me for bread
I will give him diamonds instead.

MARY DIXON THAYER

I Keep Three Wishes Ready

I keep three wishes ready,
Lest I should chance to meet,
Any day a fairy
Coming down the street.

I'd hate to have to stammer,
Or have to think them out,
For it's very hard to think things up
When a fairy is about.

And I'd hate to lose my wishes,
For fairies fly away,
And perhaps I'd never have a chance
On any other day.

So I keep three wishes ready,
Lest I should chance to meet,
Any day a fairy
Coming down the street.

ANNETTE WYNNE

The Falling Star

I saw a star slide down the sky,
Blinding the north as it went by,
Too lovely to be bought or sold,
Too burning and too quick to hold,
Good only to make wishes on
And then forever to be gone.

SARA TEASDALE

After All and After All

Dreaming of a prince
Cinderella sat among the ashes long ago;
Dreaming of a prince,
She scoured the pots and kettles till they shone;
        and so,
After all and after all,
Gaily at the castle ball
Cinderella met her prince long and long ago.

Dreaming of a prince
Sleeping Beauty lay in happy slumber, white
        and still;
Dreaming of a prince,
She waited for a hundred years and then his
        bugles shrill,
After all and after all,
Woke the castle, bower, and hall,
And he found her waiting for him long and
        long ago.

Dreaming of a prince
I polish bowl and teapot and the spoons, each
        one;
Dreaming of a prince,
I hang the new-washed clothes to wave
        a-drying in the sun;
After all and after all,
Great adventures may befall
Like to those that happened once long and
        long ago.

MARY CAROLYN DAVIES

118

The Shiny Little House

I wish, how I wish, that I had a little house,
With a mat for the cat and a hole for a mouse,
And a clock going "tock" in a corner of the
 room
And a kettle, and a cupboard, and a big birch
 broom.

To school in the morning the children off
 would run,
And I'd give them a kiss and a penny and a
 bun.
But directly they had gone from this little house
 of mine,
I'd clasp my hands and snatch a cloth, and
 shine, shine, shine.

I'd shine all the knives, all the windows and
 the floors,
All the grates, all the plates, all the handles on
 the doors,
Every fork, every spoon, every lid, and every
 tin,
Till everything was shining like a new bright
 pin.

At night, by the fire, when the children were
 in bed,
I'd sit and I'd knit, with a cap upon my head,
And the kettles, and the saucepans they would
 shine, shine, shine,
In this tweeny, little, cosy little house of mine.

NANCY M. HAYES

Hold Fast Your Dreams

Hold fast your dreams!
Within your heart
Keep one still, secret spot
Where dreams may go,
And sheltered so,
May thrive and grow—
Where doubt and fear are not.
Oh, keep a place apart
Within your heart,
For little dreams to go.

LOUISE DRISCOLL

If No One Ever Marries Me

If no one ever marries me
   I shan't mind very much;
I shall buy a squirrel in a cage
   And a little rabbit-hutch;

I shall have a cottage near a wood,
   And a pony all my own,
And a little lamb quite clean and tame
   That I can take to town:

And when I'm getting really old,
   — At twenty-eight or nine —
I shall buy a little orphan-girl
   And bring her up as mine.

LAWRENCE ALMA-TADEMA

119

Otherwise

There must be magic,
Otherwise,
How could day turn to night,

And how could sailboats,
Otherwise,
Go sailing out of sight,

And how could peanuts,
Otherwise,
Be covered up so tight?

AILEEN FISHER

General Store

Some day I'm going to have a store
With a tinkly bell hung over the door,
With real glass cases and counters wide
And drawers all spilly with things inside.
There'll be a little of everything;
Bolts of calico; balls of string;
Jars of peppermint; tins of tea;
Pots and kettles and crockery;
Seeds in packets; scissors bright;
Kegs of sugar, brown and white;
Sarsaparilla for picnic lunches,
Bananas and rubber boots in bunches.
I'll fix the window and dust each shelf,
And take the money in all myself,
It will be my store and I will say:
"What can I do for you to-day?"

RACHEL FIELD

Bunches of Grapes

"Bunches of grapes," says Timothy;
    "Pomegranates pink," says Elaine;
"A junket of cream and a cranberry tart
    For me," says Jane.

"Love-in-a-mist," says Timothy;
    "Primroses pale," says Elaine;
"A nosegay of pinks and mignonette
    For me," says Jane.

"Chariots of gold," says Timothy;
    "Silvery wings," says Elaine;
"A bumpity ride in a wagon of hay
    For me," says Jane.

WALTER DE LA MARE

The Peddler's Caravan

I wish I lived in a caravan
With a horse to drive, like the peddler-man!
Where he comes from nobody knows,
Or where he goes to, but on he goes!

His caravan has windows two,
And a chimney of tin, that the smoke comes
    through;
He has a wife, with a baby brown,
And they go riding from town to town.

Chairs to mend and delf to sell!
He clashes the basins like a bell;
Tea-trays, baskets ranged to order,
Plates, with alphabets round the border!

The roads are brown, and the sea is green,
But his house is like a bathing machine;
The world is round, and he can ride,
Rumble and slash, to the other side!

With the peddler-man I should like to roam,
And write a book when I get home;
All the people would read my book,
Just like the Travels of Captain Cook!

WILLIAM BRIGHTY RANDS

Trades

I want to be a carpenter,
To work all day long in clean wood,
Shaving it into little thin slivers
Which screw up into curls behind my plane;
Pounding square, black nails into white
    boards,
With the claws of my hammer glistening
Like the tongue of a snake.
I want to shingle a house,
Sitting on the ridge-pole in a bright breeze.
I want to put the shingles on neatly,
Taking great care that each is directly between
    two others.

I want my hands to have the tang of wood:
Spruce, Cedar, Cypress.
I want to draw a line on a board with a flat
    pencil,
And then saw along that line,
With the sweet-smelling sawdust piling up in
    a yellow heap at my feet.

That is the life!
Heigh-ho!
It is much easier than to write this poem.

AMY LOWELL

Wishing

Ring—ting! I wish I were a primrose,
A bright yellow primrose blooming in the
     spring!
  The stooping boughs above me,
  The wandering bee to love me,
The fern and moss to creep across,
And the elm tree for our king!

Nay—stay! I wish I were an elm tree,
A great, lofty elm tree with green leaves gay!
  The winds would set them dancing,
  The sun and moonshine glance in,
The birds would house among the boughs,
And ever sweetly sing!

Oh—no! I wish I were a robin,
A robin or a little wren, everywhere to go;
  Through forest, field, or garden,
  And ask no leave or pardon,
Till winter comes with icy thumbs
To ruffle up our wings!

Well—tell! Where should I fly to,
Where go to sleep in the dark wood or dell?
  Before a day was over,
  Home comes the rover,
For Mother's kiss—sweeter this
Than any other thing.

WILLIAM ALLINGHAM

122

COMES THE STARLIGHTER

The Children's Hour

Between the dark and the daylight,
 When the night is beginning to lower,
Comes a pause in the day's occupations,
 That is known as the Children's Hour.

I hear in the chamber above me
 The patter of little feet,
The sound of a door that is opened,
 And voices soft and sweet.

From my study I see in the lamplight,
 Descending the broad hall stair,
Grave Alice, and laughing Allegra,
 And Edith with golden hair.

A whisper, and then a silence:
 Yet I know by their merry eyes
They are plotting and planning together
 To take me by surprise.

A sudden rush from the stairway,
 A sudden raid from the hall!
By three doors left unguarded
 They enter my castle wall!

They climb up into my turret
 O'er the arms and back of my chair;
If I try to escape, they surround me;
 They seem to be everywhere.

They almost devour me with kisses,
 Their arms about me entwine,
Till I think of the Bishop of Bingen
 In his Mouse-Tower on the Rhine!

Do you think, O blue-eyed banditti,
 Because you have scaled the wall,
Such an old mustache as I am
 Is not a match for you all!

I have you fast in my fortress,
 And will not let you depart,
But put you down into the dungeon
 In the round-tower of my heart.

And there will I keep you forever,
 Yes, forever and a day,
Till the walls shall crumble to ruin,
 And moulder in dust away!

HENRY WADSWORTH LONGFELLOW

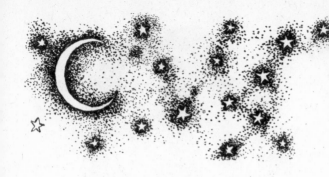

Light the Lamps Up, Lamplighter

*For a lamplighter, A Grandmother, The Angel
Gabriel And Any Number of Others.*

Light the lamps up, Lamplighter,
   The people are in the street—
     Without a light
     They have no sight,
And where will they plant their feet?
Some will tread in the gutter,
And some in the mud—Oh dear!
Light the lamps up, Lamplighter,
Because the night is here.

Light the candles, Grandmother,
The children are going to bed—
     Without a wick
     They'll stumble and stick,
And where will they lay their head?
Some will lie on the staircase,
And some in the hearth—Oh dear!
Light the candles, Grandmother,
Because the night is here.

Light the stars up, Gabriel,
The cherubs are out to fly—
     If heaven is blind
     How will they find
Their way across the sky?
Some will splash in the Milky Way,
Or bump on the moon—Oh, dear!
Light the stars up, Gabriel,
Because the night is here.

ELEANOR FARJEON

Bedtime

All day in Mother's garden here
I play and play and play.
But when night brings a dozen stars
I can no longer stay.

Sometimes the sun has hardly set
Before the stars begin.
A dozen stars come out so fast
And then I must go in.

I count them very carefully,
Especially 'round the moon,
Because I do not wish to go
To bed a star too soon.

HELEN COALE CREW

The Stars In Town

At the seashore last week they showed me the
    stars,
And taught me the names of a few,
And the patterns they made, with their
    spangles of gold,
On a sky that was darker than blue.

When we strolled after supper to-night in the
    Park,
As I sometimes may do for a treat,
The very same stars—oh, I jumped with
    surprise—
Shone high over housetop and street.

The Dipper was there, and the zigzag-y Chair,
And the Star of the North looking down.
At the seashore, I wonder, what shines in the
    place
Of the stars that have moved into town?

MARIANA GRISWOLD VAN RENSSELAER

The Moon's The North Wind's Cooky

The Moon's the North Wind's cooky,
He bites it, day by day,
Until there's but a rim of scraps
That crumble all away.

The South Wind is a baker.
He kneads clouds in his den,
And bakes a crisp new moon *that . . . greedy*
North . . . Wind . . . eats . . . again!

VACHEL LINDSAY

The Man In The Moon

The Man in the Moon as he sails the sky
Is a very remarkable skipper,
But he made a mistake when he tried to take
A drink of milk from the Dipper.
He dipped right out of the Milky Way,
And slowly and carefully filled it,
The Big Bear growled, and the Little Bear
    howled
And frightened him so that he spilled it!

OLD RHYME

February Twilight

I stood beside a hill
    Smooth with new-laid snow,
A single star looked out
    From the cold evening glow.

There was no other creature
    That saw what I could see—
I stood and watched the evening star
    As long as it watched me.

SARA TEASDALE

Questions At Night

Why
Is the sky?

What starts the thunder overhead?
Who makes the crashing noise?
Are the angels falling out of bed?
Are they breaking all their toys?

Why does the sun go down so soon?
Why do the night-clouds crawl
Hungrily up to the new-laid moon
And swallow it, shell and all?

If there's a bear among the stars,
As all the people say,
Won't he jump over those pasture-bars
And drink up the milky way?

Does every star that happens to fall
Turn into a firefly?
Can't it ever get back to Heaven at all?
And why
Is the sky?

LOUIS UNTERMEYER

Night

Stars over snow,
    And in the west a planet
Swinging below a star—
    Look for a lovely thing and
        you will find it,
It is not far—
    It never will be far.

SARA TEASDALE

Mockery

Happened that the moon was up before I went
    to bed,
Poking through the bramble trees her round
    gold head.
   I didn't stop for stocking,
I didn't stop for shoe,
But went running out to meet her—oh, the
    night was blue!

Barefoot down the hill road, dust beneath my
    toes;
Barefoot in the pasture smelling sweet of fern
    and rose!
   Oh, night was running with me,
Tame folk were all in bed—
And the moon was just showing her wild gold
    head.

But before I reached the hilltop where the
    bramble trees are tall,
I looked to see my lady moon—she wasn't there
    at all!—
   Not sitting on the hilltop,
Nor slipping through the air,
Nor hanging in the brambles by her bright
    gold hair!

I walked slowly down the pasture and slowly
    up the hill,
Wondering and wondering, and very, very
    still.
   I wouldn't look behind me,
I went at once to bed—
And poking through the window was her bold
    gold head!

KATHERINE DIXON RIGGS

127

The Fairy Book

When Mother takes the Fairy Book
    And we curl up to hear,
'Tis "All aboard for Fairyland!"
    Which seems to be so near.

For soon we reach the pleasant place
    Of Once Upon a Time,
Where birdies sing the hour of day,
    And flowers talk in rhyme;

Where Bobby is a velvet Prince,
    And where I am a Queen;
Where one can talk with animals,
    And walk about unseen;

Where Little People live in nuts,
    And ride on butterflies,
And wonders kindly come to pass
    Before your very eyes;

Where candy grows on every bush,
    And playthings on the trees,
And visitors pick basketfuls
    As often as they please.

It is the nicest time of day—
    Though bedtime is so near,—
When Mother takes the Fairy Book
    And we curl up to hear.

ABBIE FARWELL BROWN

The Sleepy Song

As soon as the fire burns red and low,
And the house up-stairs is still,
She sings me a queer little sleepy song,
Of sheep that go over a hill.

The good little sheep run quick and soft,
Their colors are gray and white:
They follow their leader nose to tail,
For they must be home by night.

And one slips over and one comes next,
And one runs after behind,
The gray one's nose at the white one's tail,
The top of the hill they find.

And when they get to the top of the hill
They quietly slip away,
But one runs over and one comes next—
Their colors are white and gray.

And over they go, and over they go,
And over the top of the hill,
The good little sheep run quick and soft,
And the house up-stairs is still.

And one slips over and one comes next,
The good little, gray little sheep!
I watch how the fire burns red and low,
And she says that I fall asleep.

JOSEPHINE DASKAM BACON

Green Moth

The night the green moth came for me,
  A creamy moon poured down the hill,
The meadow seemed a silver sea,
Small pearls were hung in every tree,
  And all so still, so still.

He floated in on my white bed,
  A strange and soundless fellow.
I saw the horns wave on his head,
  He stepped across my pillow
In tiny ermine boots, and spread
  His cape of green and yellow.

He came so close that I could see
  His golden eyes, and sweet and chill,
His faint breath wavered over me.
"Come Child, my Beautiful," said he,
  And all so still, so still.

WINIFRED WELLES

Night Magic

(A Lie-awake Song)

The apples falling from the tree
Make such a heavy bump at night
I always am surprised to see
They are so little, when it's light;

And all the dark just sings and sings
So loud, I cannot see at all
How frogs and crickets and such things
That make the noise, can be so small.

Then my own room looks larger, too—
Corners so dark and far away—
I wonder if things really do
Grow up at night and shrink by day?

For I dream sometimes, just as clear,
I'm bigger than the biggest men—
Then mother says, "Wake up, my dear!"
And I'm a little boy again.

AMELIA JOSEPHINE BURR

129

Check

The Night was creeping on the ground!
She crept and did not make a sound,

Until she reached the tree: And then
She covered it, and stole again

Along the grass beside the wall!
—I heard the rustling of her shawl

As she threw blackness everywhere
Along the sky, the ground, the air,

And in the room where I was hid!
But, no matter what she did

To everything that was without,
She could not put my candle out!

So I stared at the Night! And she
Stared back solemnly at me!

JAMES STEPHENS

The Chirrupy Cricket

There's a chirrupy cricket as guest in my room;
He's quiet all day, but at night in the gloom,
With a *zip* on the hearth and a *zup* at the door,
The chirrupy cricket hops out on the floor.

He's black and he's shiny, he's not very fat,
He's sleek as the silk of my father's tall hat;
He skates and skeedaddles on carpet and rug,
And seems an extremely well-bred little bug.

And when I'm alone in my room every night,
And the shadows have come, and the moon's
        out of sight,
And the world is all silent and solemn and bare,
I'm glad that my chirrupy cricket is there!

MARTHA B. THOMAS

Escape At Bedtime

The lights from the parlor and kitchen shone
        out
    Through the blinds and the windows and
        bars;
And high overhead and all moving about,
    There were thousands of millions of stars.
There ne'er were such thousands of leaves on
        a tree,
    Nor of people in church or the Park,
As the crowds of the stars that looked down
        upon me,
    And that glittered and winked in the dark.

The Dog, and the Plow, and the Hunter,
        and all,
    And the star of the sailor, and Mars,
These shone in the sky, and the pail by the wall
    Would be half full of water and stars.
They saw me at last, and they chased me with
        cries,
    And they soon had me packed into bed;
But the glory kept shining and bright in my
        eyes,
    And the stars going round in my head.

ROBERT LOUIS STEVENSON

At Night

When I go to bed at night
The darkness is a bear.
He crouches in the corner,
Or hides behind a chair;
The one who tells me stories—
She does not know he's there.

But when she kisses me good-night,
And darkness starts to creep
Across the floor, why, then I see
It's just a woolly sheep,
That nibbles at my rugs awhile
Before we go to sleep.

ANNE BLACKWELL PAYNE

The Plumpuppets

When little heads weary have gone to their
    bed,
When all the good nights and the prayers have
    been said,
Of all the good fairies that send bairns to rest
The Little Plumpuppets are those I love best.

If your pillow is lumpy, or hot, thin, and flat,
The little Plumpuppets know just what
    they're at:
They plump up the pillow, all soft, cool,
    and fat—
    The little Plumpuppets plump-up it!

The little Plumpuppets are fairies of beds;
They have nothing to do but to watch sleepy-
    heads;
They turn down the sheets and they tuck you
    in tight,
And they dance on your pillow to wish you
    good night!

No matter what troubles have bothered the
    day,
Though your doll broke her arm or the pup
    ran away;
Though your handies are black with the ink
    that was spilt—
Plumpuppets are waiting in blanket and quilt.

If your pillow is lumpy, or hot, thin, and flat,
The little Plumpuppets know just what
    they're at;
They plump up the pillow, all soft, cool, and
    fat—
    The little Plumpuppets plump-up it!

                    CHRISTOPHER MORLEY

Two In Bed

       When my brother Tommy
       Sleeps in bed with me,
        He doubles up
        And makes
         himself
         exactly
         like
         a
         V

And 'cause the bed is not so wide,
A part of him is on my side.

                    A. B. ROSS

Grown Up

Was it for this I uttered prayers,
And sobbed and cursed
And kicked the stairs,
That now, domestic as a plate,
I should retire at half-past eight!

            EDNA ST. VINCENT MILLAY

131

Lullaby, oh, lullaby!
Flowers are closed and lambs are sleeping;
Lullaby, oh, lullaby!
Stars are up, the moon is peeping;
Lullaby, oh, lullaby!
While the birds are silence keeping,
Lullaby, oh, lullaby!
Sleep, my baby, fall a-sleeping,
Lullaby, oh, lullaby!

CHRISTINA ROSSETTI

Cradle Song

From groves of spice,
O'er fields of rice,
Athwart the lotus stream,
I bring for you,
A-glint with dew,
A little lovely dream.

Sweet, shut your eyes,
The wild fireflies
Dance through the fairy neem;
From the poppyhole
For you I stole
A little lovely dream.

Dear eyes, good night,
In golden light
The stars around you gleam;
On you I press
With soft caress
A little lovely dream.

SAROJINI NAIDU

Cradle Song

Sleep, baby, sleep!
Thy father's watching the sheep,
Thy mother's shaking the dreamland tree,
And down drops a little dream for thee.
Sleep, baby, sleep!

Sleep, baby, sleep!
The large stars are the sheep,
The little stars are the lambs, I guess,
The bright moon is the shepherdess.
Sleep, baby, sleep!

Sleep, baby, sleep!
Thy Saviour loves His sheep;
And thou His little lamb shall be,
And in His arms He will carry thee,
Sleep, baby, sleep!

ELIZABETH PRENTISS

Chinese Lullaby

Chinese Sandmen,
Wise and creepy,
Croon dream-songs
To make us sleepy.
A Chinese maid with slanting eyes
Is queen of all their lullabies.
On her ancient moon-guitar
She strums a sleep-song to a star;
And when China-shadows fall
Snow-white lilies hear her call.
Chinese sandmen,
Wise and creepy,
Croon dream-songs
To make us sleepy.

UNKNOWN

The Early Morning

The moon on the one hand, the dawn on the
    other:
The moon is my sister, the dawn is my brother.
The moon on my left and the dawn on my
    right.
My brother, good morning: my sister, good
    night.

HILAIRE BELLOC

Good Night

Good night! Good night!
Far flies the light;
But still God's love
Shall flame above,
Making all bright.
Good night! Good night!

VICTOR HUGO

INDEX OF TITLES

ACKNOWLEDGMENTS

In some cases where poems or verses are not acknowledged, the compiler has searched diligently to find sources—to get permission to use them—but without success.

For the courteous permission to use the following selections, grateful acknowledgment and thanks are extended to the following authors, publishers and periodicals.

THE AMERICAN SCANDINAVIAN FOUNDATION: "The Tree" from *Poems and Songs* by Bjornstjerne Bjornson, translated by Professor Palmer.

D. APPLETON CENTURY AND COMPANY: "The Little Elf" by John Kendrick Bangs from *St. Nicholas Book of Verse*, copyright 1923. "The Elf and the Dormouse" by Oliver Herford, copyright 1894, 1922. "The Sea Princess" by Katharine Pyle from *St. Nicholas*. "Spring" from *I Have a Song to Sing to You* by Laura E. Richards, copyright 1938.

DOROTHY W. BARUCH: "Cat" from *I Like Animals*; "Barber's Clippers," "Merry-Go-Round," and "Riding in a Motor Boat" from *I Like Machinery*; published by Harper Bros.

BASIL BLACKWELL & MOTT, LTD., OXFORD: "The Happy Sheep" by Wilfred Thorley.

BOBBS-MERRILL COMPANY: "Extremes" from *The Book of Joyous Children* by James Whitcomb Riley, copyright 1902, 1930.

BOOKHOUSE FOR CHILDREN: "The Circus Parade" and "The Road to China" from *My Book House* by Olive Beaupre Miller; "Lilies," "The Rains of Spring" and "A Shower" from *My Travel Ship* by Olive Beaupre Miller.

BRANDT & BRANDT: "Grown Up" and "Portrait by a Neighbor" from *A Few Figs from Thistles* by Edna St. Vincent Millay, copyright 1921.

CHILD LIFE: "If You've Never" by Elsie M. Fowler. "Her Choice" and "A Lovely Bed" by Mattie Lee Hausgen. "The Sea Gull" by Leroy F. Jackson. "Hallowe'en" by Anna Medary. "Thanksgiving" by Margaret Munsterberg. "Swimming" by Clinton Scollard. "Camp Chums," "Welcome," and "Sing-Time" by Rose Waldo.

CHRISTIAN SCIENCE MONITOR: "Which?" by Joyce L. Brisley. "Jack Frost" by Helen Bayley Davis.

THE CHURCHMAN: "The Twenty-Fourth of December."

THE COMMONWEAL: "Juniper" by Eileen Duggan. "Godmother" by Phyllis B. Morden.

STATE OF CONNECTCUT: "Fun in a Garret" by Emma C. Dowd.

COWARD-McCANN, INC.: "The Barn," "The Mouse" and "To Think!" from *Compass Rose* by Elizabeth Coatsworth, copyright 1929.

DODD, MEAD & COMPANY, INC.: "A Vagabond Song" from *Bliss Carman Poems*, copyright 1929. "I Meant To Do My Work Today" from *The Lonely Dancer* by Richard LeGallienne, copyright 1913; and "A Song of Bread and Honey" from *New Poems* by Richard LeGallienne. "Cradle Song" from *The Golden Threshold* by Sarojini Naidu.

DOUBLEDAY & COMPANY, INC.: "Night Magic" from *Heart Awake* by Amelia Josephine Burr, copyright 1919. "The Willows" from *Echoes and Realities* by Walter Prichard Eaton, copyright 1918. "At the Theater," "General Store," and "Vegetables" from *Taxis and Toadstools* by Rachel Field, copyright 1926. "Vision" from *The Fairy Green* by Rose Fyleman, copyright 1923; "Very Lovely" and "The Child Next Door" from *Fairies and Chimneys* by Rose Fyleman, copyright 1920; "Shop Windows" from *Gay Go Up* by Rose Fyleman, copyright 1929. "Easter" from *Poems, Essays and Letters* by Joyce Kilmer, copyright 1914, 1917, 1918; "The House With Nobody In It," from *Trees and Other Poems* by Joyce Kilmer, copyright 1914. "The Blackbird" from *Kensington Gardens* by Humbert Wolfe.

GERALD DUCKWORTH & CO. LTD.: "The Early Morning" by Hilaire Belloc.

E. P. DUTTON & CO., INC.: "Galoshes," "Icy," "Snowstorm," and "Under the Ground" from *Stories to Begin On* by Rhoda W. Bacmeister, copyright 1940. "The Donkey" from *The Wild Knight and Other Poems* by G. K. Chesterton. "Little White Lily" from *Poems* by George MacDonald, copyright, 1887. "Jump or Jiggle" by Evelyn Beyer, "Little Black Bug" by Margaret Wise Brown, "Mirrors" and "Aeroplane" by Mary McB. Green, "The House of the Mouse" by Lucy Sprague Mitchell, "Snow on the Roof" and "My Bed" by Elizabeth Manson Scott, and "There Are So Many Ways of Going Places" by Leslie Thompson, from *Another Here and Now Story Book*, compiled by Lucy Sprague Mitchell, copyright 1937. "The Edge of the World" from *When We Were Little (Children's Rhymes of Oyster Bay)* by Mary Fanny Youngs, copyright 1919, renewed 1947.

FOLLETT PUBLISHING COMPANY: "A Modern Dragon," "Pussy Willows," "Shell Castles," and "The Zeppelin" from *Songs From Around a Toadstool Table* by Rowena Bastin Bennett, copyright 1930, 1937.

HARCOURT, BRACE AND COMPANY, INC.: "Hearth" from *Animosities* by Peggy Bacon, copyright 1931. "Questions at Night" from *Rainbow in the Sky* by Louis Untermeyer, copyright 1935. "The Invisible Playmate" and "The Faithless Flowers" from *Little Girl and Boy Land* by Margaret Widdemer, copyright 1924.

HARPER & BROTHERS: "My Zipper Suit" and "Sneezing" from *Pocketful of Rhymes* by Mary Louis Allen, copyright 1939. "Autumn Woods," "Ducks at Dawn," and "Circus Parade" from *A World To Know* by James S. Tippett, copyright 1933; and "Familiar Friends" from *I Spend the Summer* by James S. Tippett, copyright 1930.

HENRY HOLT AND COMPANY, INC.: "Martha," "The Cupboard," and "Bunches of Grapes" from *Collected Poems* by Walter de la Mare, copyright 1920. "The Pasture" from *Collected Poems of Robert Frost*, copyright 1930, 1939 by Henry Holt and Company, Inc.; copyright 1936 by Robert Frost. "Theme in Yellow" from *Chicago Poems* by Carl Sandburg, copyright 1916 by Henry Holt and Company, Inc.; copyright 1943 by Carl Sandburg.

HOUGHTON MIFFLIN COMPANY: "Marjorie's Almanac" by Thomas Bailey Aldrich. "The Fairy Book" from *Pocketful of Posies* by Abbie Farwell Brown. "A Rabbit" from *Little Freckled Person* by Mary Carolyn Davies. "The Wagon in the Barn" from *All About Me* by John Drinkwater. "The Christmas Tree in the Nursery," by Richard Watson Gilder. "The Children's Hour" by Henry Wadsworth Longfellow. "Sea Shell" from *Dome of Many Coloured Glass* and "Trades" from *Pictures of the Floating World* by Amy Lowell. "An Indignant Male" by A. B. Ross from *Very Young Verses*. "The Snowbird" from *Little Folk Lyrics* by Frank Dempster Sherman. "The Sandpiper" by Celia Thaxter.

ALICE HUBBARD: "The Ducks," "The Leaves Drink," "Little Brown Bear," "New Shoes," and "Ways of Traveling" by Alice Wilkins from *The Golden Flute*, published by the John Day Company.

Bruce Humphries, Inc.: "New Shoes" from *Do You Remember* by Marjorie Seymour Watts, copyright 1927 by Four Seas Company.

Marshall Jones Company: "The Little Red Sled" by Jocelyn Bush from *The Child's Own Book of Letters and Stories.*

Junior High School Division, Brooklyn: "April" by Evelyn Stockman from *Moments of Enchantment.*

Alfred A. Knopf, Inc.: "November Night" from *Verse* by Adelaide Crapsey, copyright 1915 by Algernon S. Crapsey; in 1934 by Adelaide T. Crapsey. "Little Brother's Secret" from *Poems* by Katherine Mansfield, copyright 1924. "Overtones" from *The Collected Poems of William Alexander Percy*, copyright 1920 and 1943 by LeRoy Pratt Percy. "The Locust" from the story "The Coyote and the Locust" in *Zuni Folk Tales* by Frank Cushing, copyright 1931.

Ladies' Home Journal: "The Best Time of All" by Nancy Byrd Turner, copyright 1926.

John Lane, the Bodley Head, Ltd.: "The First Tooth" and "The Peddler's Caravan" from *Lilliput Lyrics* by William Brighty Rands. "How the Flowers Grow" from *The Child World* by Gabriel Setoun.

J. B. Lippincott Company: "Adventure," "Humming Bird," and "Little Snail" from *Poems by a Little Girl* by Hilda Conkling, copyright 1920; "The Cellar" from *Shoes of the Wind* by Hilda Conkling, copyright 1922. "Circus" from *Joan's Door* by Eleanor Farjeon, copyright 1926; "Jim at the Corner" from *Over the Garden Wall* by Eleanor Farjeon, copyright 1933; "Poetry" from *Sing for Your Supper* by Eleanor Farjeon, copyright 1938. "The Plumpuppets," "Song for a Little House," "Smells (Junior)" from *The Rocking Horse* by Christopher Morley, copyright 1919; "Animal Crackers" from *Songs for a Little House*, copyright 1917, 1945. "I Keep Three Wishes Ready" and "I Heard It in the Valley" from *All Through the Year* by Annette Wynne, copyright 1932; "Indian Children" and "People Buy a Lot of Things" from *For Days and Days* by Annette Wynne, copyright 1919.

Little, Brown & Company: "Apple Blossom" and "The Worm" from *Jane, Joseph and John* by Ralph Bergengren. "September" from *Sonnets and Lyrics* by Helen Hunt Jackson.

Longmans, Green & Co., Inc.: "Children, Children, Don't Forget" by Dora Owen.

The Macmillan Company: "A Memory," "A Swing Song," "The Fairies," and "Wishing" from *Robin Redbreast and Other Verses* by William Allingham. "The Hairy Dog" and "Skating" from *Phillicock Hill* by Herbert Asquith. "My Dog" from *Rhymes About Ourselves* by Marchette Gaylord Chute. "The Rabbits' Song Outside the Tavern" from *Away Goes Sally* by Elizabeth Coatsworth. "I Saw the Wind Today" from *Dramatic Legends* by Padraic Colum. "The Little Rose Tree" and "Roads" from *Pointed People* by Rachel Field. "The Little Turtle" and "The Moon's the North Wind's Cooky" from *Collected Poems* by Vachel Lindsay. "Cat" and "Shore" from *Menagerie* by Mary Britton Miller. "Hurt No Living Thing," "Lullaby," "Morning and Evening," and "Winter" from *Sing Song* by Christina Rossetti. "Check," "Little Things," and "The Snare" from *Collected Poems* by James Stephens. "At the Sea-Side" and "Escape at Bedtime" from *A Child's Garden of Verses* by Robert Louis Stevenson. "Paper Boats" from *Crescent Moon* by Rabindranath Tagore. "The Falling Star," "February Twilight" and "Night" from *Stars Tonight* by Sara Teasdale. "Invitation" from *Poems* by Ridgely Torrence. "The Angel in the Apple Tree" and "Green Moth" from *Skipping Along Alone* by Winifred Welles.

Macrae Smith Company: "The Teapot Dragon," "Foolish Flowers," "Jack-in-the-Pulpit," and "When I Grow Up" from *All Around Our House* by Rupert Sargent Holland, copyright 1919 by George W. Jacobs and Company.

Helen M. Malloch: "If Easter Eggs Would Hatch" by Douglas Malloch, copyright 1926.

Robert McBride & Company: "A Coffeepot Face" and "Otherwise" from *The Coffee-Pot Face* by Aileen Fisher.

Oxford University Press, London: "Hail on the Pine Trees" and "Willows in the Snow" from *A Year of Japanese Epigrams* by William N. Porter.

Poetry (Chicago): "Mockery" by Katherine Dixon Riggs.

The Poetry Review, Journal of the Poetry Society, Inc.: "The Scarecrow" by Michael Franklin.

Punch: "Crab-Apple" by Ethel Talbot.

G. P. Putnam's Sons: "Little" from *Everything and Anything* by Dorothy Aldis, copyright 1925, 1926, 1927; "The Grasshoppers" and "Whistles" from *Here, There and Everywhere* by Dorothy Aldis, copyright 1927, 1928; and "The Seals" from *Hop, Skip and Jump* by Dorothy Aldis, copyright 1934.

Rinehart & Company, Inc.: "Gentle Name" from *City Child* by Selma Robinson, copyright 1931.

Charles Scribner's Sons: "The Sleepy Song" from *Poems* by Josephine D. D. Bacon, copyright 1903, 1931 by Josephine D. D. Bacon. "One, Two, Three!" from *Poems* by Henry C. Bunner, copyright 1896, 1899 by Charles Scribner's Sons; 1923 by Alice Larned Bunner. "Duck's Ditty" from *The Wind in the Willows* by Kenneth Grahame, copyright 1908, 1935.

Story Parade: "Funny" by Aileen L. Fisher.

Genevieve Taggard and The New Yorker: "Millons of Strawberries."

The Viking Press, Inc.: Two "home-made jingles" from *Bequest of Wings* by Annis Duff, copyright 1944. "Christmas Morning," "The Butterbean Tent," "Little Rain," and "Mumps" from *Under the Tree* by Elizabeth Madox Roberts, copyright 1922. "Shoes" and "Woodpecker With Long Ears" from *In and Out* by Tom Robinson, copyright 1943.

Frederick Warne & Co., Inc. and Frederick Warne & Co., Ltd.: "A Tea-Party," "On the Bridge," and "Susan Blue" by Kate Greenaway.

Ann Watkins, Inc.: "Light the Lamps Up, Lamplighter," by Eleanor Farjeon.

Wheeler Publishing Company: "Bedtime" by Helen Coale Crew from *Happy Days.*

Woman's Home Companion: "The Escape" by Emily Burt.

Yale University Press: "Bundles," "Chanticleer," and "Water Lily" from *Songs for Parents* by John Farrar. "Cover" from *Hemlock Wall* by Frances Frost. "Poplars" from *Lyra Levis* and "September" from *Sea Moods* by Edward Bliss Reed.

Youth's Companion: "A Garden Path" by May Justus. "Some Things That Easter Brings" by Elsie Parrish. "Traveling Light" by Minnie Leona Upton.

2295-1